*To my husband, who gave me the opportunity and
pushed me to try.
To my kids, who inspire me daily to be better.
To my parents, who always believed that I could.*

DESTINED FOR A
LIFE UNKOWN

Jolene Gettler

ISBN 978-1-7388356-0-7 (Softcover Print)
ISBN 978-1-7388356-2-1 (Hardcover Print)
ISBN 978-1-7388356-1-4 (Electronic Book)

Cover design by GetCovers

CONTENTS

JOURNAL

I am a Traveller.

Not in the traditional way. I don't travel the world, at least not anymore. I may never again have that pleasure.

I have this amazing, unexplained, completely uncharted (as far as I know) way of travelling.

Does this sound lame? I don't know how to start this. If this does sound lame, I just wanted to say, on the record, that I think it might be.

On my seventeenth birthday, my mom gifted me this blank book and highly suggested that I start a journal, or as she phrased it, "write a memoir." (How many teenagers do you know writing a *memoir*?) When I say highly suggest, I mean she will not leave me alone and keeps nagging me about it. This book is not your typical journal. It is a heavy leather bound, the spine creaks when you open it, has a built-in ribbon bookmark, and fancy type of journal. She wants handwritten accounts of my travels, both past and present. Old-school journaling. I'm not a writer and can't describe anything to save my life, so this should be a super fun project. (Yes Mom, that was sarcasm.) So if this does sound lame, or I ramble, or if anything feels out of order, this is not my fault. This book I am being forced to write in is just too pretty to have pages ripped out of it. My mother is an Evil Genius.

She actually said, "Who knows, one day your journal could become a real book that you can purchase in a real bookstore!"

Cool Mom, I can see the cover now. The title will be "The Diary of a Deranged Teenager" with the caption "No one believes me, but maybe you will."

The back will have all the testimonials;

"Wonderfully written, with minimal attitude." – Mom.

"The best book I have ever read." – Dad

"The secondary characters are what brings this story to life." – Lotus

"I was told to read this book, and it wasn't the worst thing I ever read" – A random patient of Dad's.

I will sell maybe ten copies, two just to my parents, and a couple to some old classmates who are nosey and want to know what happened to me.

The unspoken truth is that Mom is afraid one day I will travel to a place that I love so much that I won't want to return home. I believe she silently fears that I won't be able to come back. So this journal will not only provide a written account of my gift and adventures but will also give my parents something to remember me by if any of those scenarios happen.

Well, this has turned dark fast. Moving on.

Explanation time. My travelling is hard to explain as I don't fully understand it myself. I have come to terms with it, and to simplify things, it just is what it is. Insert shrugging emoji. But I will try to explain it the best I can. First, it needs to be understood that I don't exactly travel to traditional places or destinations. It is so much more than that. I will not only end up in different places, but impossibly in different times, and perhaps maybe not even in this universe. At least I don't think so. Again, I am not sure.

Did you notice that I wrote, "end up in different places...?" I actually have no control over my travelling. I don't get to pick where I go, or when I go. I have learned to accept this and have recently started to enjoy my time away, which is good because as I have gotten older, I have been travelling more often, and for longer periods of time. My life is a bit chaotic but I have started to finally see the beauty in it.

I feel I am not making sense. If I am to give this journal a proper try, I guess I should start from the beginning, like how most stories begin.

THE BEGINNING

My family used to live in the city, and I loved it. I lived in the city of Toronto, but my friends and I just call it the city. I loved the hustle and bustle of busy sidewalks, the congested traffic and the endless amount of people coming and going from different destinations. I found the horn honking and rude gestures amusing if I even noticed them at all. The tall shiny buildings made me happy. The food! You can eat from almost anywhere in the world if you know the right places to go. Shopping, concerts, sports teams to cheer on, and festivals. If you were bored in the city, it was your fault.

My mother was a lawyer. A good one I was told, the best of the best. She was top of her class in law school and was so impressive, she made partner early into her career. She never talked a lot about her work with me, but would always tell me when she won a case, and that seemed to happen all of the time. It was my impression that you wanted her on your side, and feared her if she wasn't. She was impressive in and out of the courtroom. Her looks alone were enough to intimidate anyone. My mom is tall, five-foot-ten, which has never stopped her from wearing the most impressive designer heels to work every day. She owned and wore designer everything; Clothes, shoes, jewellery, makeup, and handbags. Her nails always looked freshly done in a simple, yet elegant, trendy manicure. She had the most impossibly beautiful natural auburn hair anyone had ever seen. Many have tried and failed to dye their hair her colour. She had it cut in what she called a professional length, with the tips teasing but never touching her shoulders. I think even her name is strong and impressive, Gwendolyn. It demands attention and respect. No one would ever dare try to shorten it or give her a cutesy nickname. Well, no one but my Dad. He calls her Gwen. He is one of her only weaknesses, myself being the other.

My father, Eric, was an ER doctor. A good one I was told. Like my mom, he never really discussed work with me, only a few happy stories here and there. I just knew that he worked hard, and worked all the time. My dad was six-foot-three, had dark shiny black hair, perfect teeth, and was lean and muscular. When he wasn't at work he was in our home gym lifting weights or running on the treadmill. My friends would always ask if my Dad was home when they came over to play. They would tell me he was better looking than most of the doctors on TV, which I found completely gross and inappropriate. As I got a little older I would see that it wasn't just my friends swooning over my dad, but their moms too. Ew. All this didn't matter to him. He only had eyes for my mom.

My parents met in such a classic, meet-cute way. It was early into both of their careers. My mom was at the hospital with a client. She wouldn't tell me the specifics of how or why she and her client were there, as she rarely does. It was a rainy spring day, one of those days where you just can't keep the floors clean with everyone coming in and out of the building, with their wet and muddy footwear. That did not stop my mom from wearing her heels, as nothing did. When she was leaving the hospital she slipped on the wet floor in a high-traffic, crowded common area. Apparently, her briefcase went flying, both of her feet found air, she lost a shoe, and her arms were flailing frantically to find something to hold onto. She said the whole thing felt like slow motion. Her arms did manage to find something to stop her fall. They landed around my dad's neck as he caught her. It was fate. He wasn't scheduled to work that day but had been called in. He walked in just in time to see Mom struggling with gravity and was able to catch her in time. Their eyes met, and I guess all the stars aligned and it was love at first sight. Today, Mom still laughs about it and says that it was a good thing Dad is so handsome, as it stopped her from suing the ass off of that place. I think she would have too. She doesn't like to be embarrassed.

They were engaged and married within a year, exchanging their vows on a beautiful spring, rainy day. They were a total power couple. Two years later, I came into the picture.

I was born on a rainy morning, May the fifteenth, with bright blond hair, brown eyes (I never had that standard baby blue most babies are born with) and chubby everything. I lost the chubby everything but kept my bright golden blond hair and whisky-brown coloured eyes. My parents have no idea where the golden locks came from. I was always a little sad that my hair never matched my mom's, but I did inherit her porcelain skin.

From my dad, I got my eye shape and his laugh. I was doomed to be tall thanks to both parents. Yes, doomed. I was an early bloomer, so it wasn't fun towering over both girls and boys at school. My mom told me that boys would eventually catch up and that I should be proud of my height like she was. As I got older, I started to care less about it.

It has been six years since we lived in the city. I have a pretty decent memory of my early youth and am not competently naive. During this time, I was only a small child, but I remember that I had it good. My parents had money, and I am an only child. I had a nanny from birth, and I went to a private school. It sounds lonely but it wasn't. My nanny was everything to me, Mrs. McKenzie. She was loving but strict. Other kids I knew had cute pet names for their nannies, but not me. I was instructed to call her Mrs. McKenzie before I could even speak. She was short and sort of round. She had a mop of curly dark grey hair on top of her head that looked unmanageable, yet it perfectly suited her. She had small facial features, small brown eyes, a button nose, and a round mouth, with her cheeks always rosy. She insisted on her strict dress code, which consisted of a conservative dress that went below the knees, an apron (The apron came off when she left the house) and sensible comfortable shoes. She got me to and from where I needed to be, fed me most of my meals and usually tucked me into bed at night. I was her only job, her only priority and I felt loved.

My parents made time for me when they could. We would always try to have a couple of dinners a week together as a family and we went on many wonderful vacations. I got to spend a lot of one-on-one time with

Mom or Dad because their days off rarely coincided. I looked forward to this just as much as being with both of them together.

Dad would take me to whatever sporting event was in town and I would cheer on whoever he was cheering for. We would wear matching jerseys and he would let me buy those obnoxious foam hands with the team's logo, that I would wave around trying to get my face on the jumbotron. After the game, we would grab what he liked to call "Street meat" which was a hotdog you buy from someone working a hotdog cart on the street corner. He would then make me promise not to tell my mom about the street meat, instead telling her we went for a healthy meal.

Mom would take me shopping. I wore a uniform to school, but she made sure I had the most up-to-date wardrobe a kid could ever want. We would get mani-pedis and have fancy lunches. She would ask me about my friends, boys, and school, make sure I was happy with Mrs. McKenzie, and ask what I actually ate for lunch when I was out last with Dad. There is no keeping any secrets from this woman.

My parents and Mrs. McKenzie kept me so busy with day trips, play dates, birthday parties, and activities, that I honestly never had time to think about how little time I spent with my parents as a complete family. When the thoughts did creep in and I started to feel a little sad, my parents always found a way to spend a day with me.

With my perfect power couple parents and a strict and loving nanny, I wouldn't have traded in my life for anything. Life was good, great, honestly perfect, for at least the first eight years.

MY BEST FRIEND

My best friend's name is Lotus. I will mention her a lot throughout my journal, as she was, and is, an important part of my life, so I felt she deserves a proper introduction.

First, I will address her name, because most people think it sounds pretty, but are also thinking to themselves, "What the F-word," or "What was her mom smoking when she named her?" Their thinking is not far off.

Lotus' mom....how do I write this without sounding... is very impressionable. It is actually kind of sad. I don't think she truly knows herself anymore, or ever has, or what she actually likes. Lotus' dad is some hotshot important banker and works with money all day, so Lotus' mom stayed home to raise her, and to find herself. When she was pregnant with Lotus, she had fallen into a hippie yoga group while trying to find a gentle exercise to do. She didn't just join the group, she fell deep into the culture. She went from eating expensive steak dinners to becoming an overnight vegan. She made herself a yoga meditation shrine in her house, burned incense around the house, and tried to recruit the other moms and caregivers at school pickup to join her new vegan lifestyle. When it came time to name Lotus, she was named after a yoga pose.

Her mom has not done yoga since Lotus was born and has gone back to her meat-eating ways. She has gone through many "life-changing" programs and phases since then. I think currently the trap she is in now is some pyramid selling scheme where makeup and skincare are involved. She is always trying to get her friends to either buy stuff from her or sell it for her. She doesn't need the money, but is bored, and needs a purpose.

Lotus and I met on the first day of preschool. Growing up, and to this day, she has been shorter than me. She has darker skin, big blue eyes, and naturally curly crazy hair, which she used to complain about it being unmanageable. I always thought she resembled Emma Watson as Hermione Granger in the first Harry Potter film. In time, she has been able to manage it and be the envy of most girls.

We instantly got along because Lotus is brutally honest and I always saw the value in that. In a way, I envied her. She knew who she was from a very young age. She was confident and didn't need to be loved or liked by people she didn't care about. Other kids thought her to be mean or rude. I saw someone who knew who she was, and what she liked, and didn't accept anything less than what she deserved. I was always quiet and reserved, so I think we balanced each other out quite well. It made me feel special to be her friend, but she always told me she felt the same way about me. Did I mention she was humble?

We have been inseparable since school started, even now, through distance and circumstance.

MY FIRST TIME

The first time I travelled, I was nine. It was early October. I remember because we were making Halloween crafts in class, and everyone was excitedly talking to each other about what costumes we had picked out for Halloween, in between cutting, glueing and colouring construction paper.

It is a bit of a blur, but from what I remember, I was talking to Lotus about my scary witch costume my mom was helping me put together when I started feeling a little dizzy. I blinked and then found myself somewhere else. I mean completely somewhere else and impossibly in another time.

I found myself outside. It was so sunny that I had to shield my eyes for a moment to get used to the natural bright light. The air was warm, and smelled so fresh and clean, compared to the cold damp fall weather we had been experiencing for weeks. I was in an open field, surrounded by beautiful gardens and flowering trees. I knew immediately that I was not anywhere in the city. I couldn't be. My parents have taken me to all the sites our city has to offer and I have never been anywhere like this at home. After a brief moment of awe and bewilderment, as I was looking around I finally realized that I wasn't alone. There were children around my age everywhere, laughing and playing. I stood frozen watching them, for how long, I am not sure. Nothing made sense, but there was so much joy around me that I couldn't possibly feel afraid. I felt confused, but that seemed to quickly fade from the joyous infection all around me. The girls were dressed so lovely in long frilly dresses and hair down in long wavy locks or tied up with ribbons. The boys looked funny to me, all in proper trousers with tucked-in funny shirts. No boy at school would be caught wearing anything like that, which is saying something, as we all wore a uniform. That is when I looked down to compare my uniform to their different attire, and I realized I was dressed just as lovely as the girls. I was wearing a very light blush pink dress, with a beautiful darker pink ribbon around my waist. The dress went almost to the ground and had a bit of lace at the hem and on my short sleeves. That was when I started to panic a little. I don't remember changing. How did I get these clothes? Whose were they? Who dressed me? Breathing was starting to get a bit hard and I found my head starting to spin, when another girl grabbed my hand and pulled me into the crowd of laughing, playing children.

She spun me around and around as she laughed with her head back, face towards the sky with her eyes closed. I copied her, and we spun for what felt like minutes, but it was probably only a few seconds. She then let go and we both went crashing to the ground, giggling at how dizzy we were. When I stood up and got myself sorted, a different girl grabbed my hands and we took a turn together spinning and letting go. This went on for a while, taking turns with different girls and boys. One boy kept coming back to me for a turn, and I found myself drawn to him as well. He was cute. He was taller than me, with dark curly hair and eyes so dark, they could be mistaken as black. They were beautiful. We didn't exchange any words, just laughter, and after a few turns together, I lost sight of him in the crowd and never saw him again.

When we all finished our spinning game, I got the first indication that there were adults present. Off in the distance, we heard a man's boisterous voice calling to all the children. We followed his voice up a slight hill to another flat clearing. I found myself frozen in awe once again. It was a grand scene. Picture every beloved period piece movie you have ever watched, that included balls, promenades, and fancy dinners. Where you get sucked into the romance of the era of ladies and gentlemen courting each other, all while blissfully ignoring the fact that they had no plumbing and that women were property, and had no rights.

Waiting for us underneath huge white open tents were three long tables filled with food. One table consisted of various loaves of bread, cheese and fruit. The second table had a roasted pig right on the table, with an apple in its mouth. Surrounding it were plates of other meats and vegetables. The third table was the most impressive. There were fancy cakes, pies, pudding and piles of pastries and chocolate. Adults were walking around filling other adults' cups with what I now know to be wine or ale. We were surrounded by beautiful gardens, with perfectly trimmed hedges, and manicured lawns. Cut flowers decorated the tents, tables, and various other places that someone felt needed flowers. There was what

I guess would be a band. Off to the side, out of the way, a few men with instruments provided background music.

It wasn't the food that had me frozen in place, nor the big tents, lavish gardens or the weird out-of-date boring classical music. The backdrop to this unbelievably picturesque scene was a huge, elegant, stone castle. A freakin' castle! Now, I have seen castles before, but never one under construction, as in, just being built. As grand as this castle was, it was either not finished or a new wing was being added. This was the moment that I finally realized that I hadn't just ended up somewhere out of the city, but may have ended up somewhere in the past. Or was I in a parallel universe? I once watched a show with my dad about some super smart nerdy people who thought this could be possible. Whatever the explanation is, and to this day, I still don't have one, I knew something amazing had happened.

This was clearly a celebration of some kind. I guess you can say that I crashed their party, whoever or whatever it was for. There were so many people present, so I had gone unnoticed, blending in with the rest of the kids. I watched as most of the children ran for the sweets table, and decided to press my luck and have a turn. I had my eye on the huge plate of chocolates when I started to feel dizzy. I found a nearby chair and sat down to steady my head again. The warm, fresh breeze felt refreshing on my face. I took a moment to close my eyes, to surrender myself to the wind's healing properties. When I opened my eyes, I was home.

I was home, as in back in the city. I found myself lying in the back seat of a car, with my head on Mom's lap. Why I didn't return to school, I have no idea. I sat up, blinking, still a bit dizzy, but more confused. Mom noticed me and she seemed super shocked to see me sitting up beside her. I don't blame her, if someone just appeared beside me out of nowhere, I would be shocked too. She threw her arms around me and squeezed me tight in her arms. She kept repeating "Thank goodness, you're ok, Thank goodness, you're ok," as she rocked me in her arms. Finally, she released her death grip on me, moved her hands to my face, and asked me what happened.

I told her everything. She quietly listened, while her hands kept fussing with my face and hair. When I got to the end of my story, I remember her finally, carefully replying, "Baby, honey, Elizabeth, that sounds like a wonderful story, but you don't really believe that this happened, do you? That you "travelled?" It just couldn't have happened. It's impossible."

I remember feeling deflated. How could she not believe me? Why would I make this up? How does she explain my disappearing from school and reappearing in her car? I have never been good at writing and storytelling. They don't even come close to the top twenty things I am good at. I'm not even good at lying. I remember crying out of frustration. To my surprise, she began to cry too.

"I'm sorry," she started. "I thought I lost you, I thought you were gone. I am just trying to understand what happened too."

After a quick phone call to Dad, we arrived at the hospital. I guess he wanted to understand how I travelled too. It turned out that many people were interested, and over the next few weeks, I saw more doctors and specialists than I care to count. The first week I was forced to stay in the hospital and wear those awful gowns that showed off my backside. After the first week, I was allowed to go home but had to return daily for more tests.

When I finished seeing all the doctors close to home, we flew to a few other places and saw even more doctors. When all the doctors were finished poking me and sending me through machines and asking me weird questions, my parents picked up my favourite takeout and brought me home. I knew they wanted to have a serious talk because they were being super nice to me, but I caught them giving each other worried looks when they thought I wouldn't notice.

They started to explain how they believed that I believed that I travelled to another place and time. I brought up the argument again about my unexplainable absence. They attempted to try to give me different explanations of what they and the doctors thought could have happened. I honestly couldn't tell you what they said. I was nine years old and pissed off that my parents were looking for another explanation other than mine, so I wasn't even listening. I know what happened.

My parents made me stay home from school for another week, after my weeks of living like a lab rat. I can only assume they were worried that I would leave again, in my new unconventional way. To be honest, at this point, no one knew if I would, or could again. Mom and Dad took turns staying home from work. I thought it would be worse to be home with the doctor, but it was Mom who fussed over me and wouldn't leave me alone. I could even hear her hovering outside the door when I used the washroom. It was a bit much. It was also a boring week. I swear it felt like I was being quarantined in the house. My friends weren't even allowed to come over. If all this wasn't bad enough, I missed Halloween at school, one of my favourite days of the year. We don't do any work, it's a huge party all day, with more candy than you can eat, and we get to ditch the uniform that day for a creepy or cool costume. It is the perfect school day. I spent it playing catch up on my schoolwork from home.

My parents did agree to let me go out trick or treating that night. On a normal year, Lotus, and a few other friends in the neighbourhood would meet at my house and one of our parents would take turns taking us around. I learned years later that the parents who got to stay behind played drinking games. They would take a shot when the most popular character that year came to the door. That year, if I can remember correctly, it would have been one of the family members from "The Incredibles" movie, or surprisingly Elsa, again, for I don't know how many years in a row. That year, there were no drinking games. I wasn't even allowed to go out with my friends. Dad walked me from house to house, alone. Every five minutes he would ask if I was feeling ok. After a half hour of his constant questions, I asked him to go home. Dad probably assumed it was from the fatigue they kept saying I had, but I was just bored and annoyed.

BACK TO NORMAL

When I was allowed to return to school I was sternly instructed not to talk about what happened with anyone, and if people kept asking, I was only allowed to say that I didn't feel well the last few weeks and was kept home. To me, that didn't make any sense. I know half the class saw me disappear from the classroom. Unbelievably, everyone bought this stupid story, except for Lotus. She saw right through my lame explanation and wouldn't talk to me for weeks out of protest. I don't blame her, best friends don't lie to each other and I was blatantly lying right to her face.

About a couple of months after "the incident" I finally convinced my parents to let me invite Lotus over for a sleepover. It took me another week to convince her to accept my invitation. I took her aside at school and told her that I would tell her the truth about everything, even though she probably would not believe it. And that is what I did. After the lights went out and we were thoroughly threatened by Mrs. McKenzie to get some sleep, I told her about my trip. She kept interrupting me to ask questions, which my parents also did and still didn't believe me, so I saw that as a bad sign, but still, I didn't leave out any details. When I was finally finished explaining my truth, we sat in silence. It probably lasted maybe a generous minute or two but it felt like hours to me. I was about to break the uncomfortable silence by telling her to forget it, when she finally looked me in the eyes and quietly said, "I believe you."

Finally, someone believed me. I felt a little less crazy that day, and it meant the world to me that it was my best friend who had my back. We made a pact (I remember we were talking about doing a blood oath, but blood can get messy, and we were pretty sure we couldn't go through with stabbing ourselves, and we conveniently didn't have a cool-looking dagger available to complete such an oath) to tell each other everything from now on, whether big or small, insignificant or not. That night bonded us for life.

The holidays came and passed without incident. I was slowly given my regular life back. My parents started to resume our regular outings, and I was able to have friends over and go out to see friends regularly. The only lasting odd behaviour came from Mrs. McKenzie. She kept trying to shove all these weird vegetables down my throat at each meal and kept trying to get me to drink this green juice that had this gross kale thing in it. She obviously had been reading too many parenting and health blogs. When I turned ten, I was allowed to host my annual birthday slumber party. I believe the theme that year was simply purple. Life was great again, perfect even.

Summer finally came to the city and the school year ended. My parents took me out for my usual end-of-the-school-year dinner, where we celebrate another passing grade, and plan our summer vacation. I had ordered my favourite baked cheesy pasta dish. I remember it smelled so good when the server placed it in front of me. Then the room spun, I closed my eyes, and I was gone.

SKIPPING SEASONS

I opened my eyes and closed them immediately, as I was met with a blast of frigid cold air. It took me a few seconds to get them fully open as I adjusted to this drastic change in temperature. It was winter. Like full-blown snowy white winter. I looked down at my clothes to see, again, I was appropriately dressed for where I was. I wore a beautiful purple coat with a huge warm hood, accompanied by light grey snow pants and purple boots. My knitted hat and mittens completed the look, which was a combo of grey and purple, with a scarf that matched. The weather was cold and I felt like I should have felt cold, but I remember being perfectly comfortable. The sun was bright, shining in a perfectly blue sky, filled with white fluffy clouds. After I got over the shock of my winter surroundings, I finally took a good look around. It looked as though I had travelled to some sort of winter carnival. It was breathtakingly beautiful. I don't think I could ever describe it properly, but I will try.

I had landed, or appeared, in the food vendor area of the carnival, so I was immediately hit with so many amazing aromas. There was hot chocolate, french fries and poutine, beavertails, pizza, popcorn, maple syrup candy, and so much more. I made a mental note to return to a few of these booths later.

When I finally got over all the food choices, my amazement shifted to the horse-drawn carriages. Families and couples were lined up for their turn to tour the carnival in the most beautiful carriages I have ever seen, pulled by the grandest horses. The carriages were decorated with tulle, ribbons and fresh flowers. The horses were dressed up to match their carriage's colour theme with similar ribbons and flowers woven or braided into their manes and tails. These horses and carriages looked like they were ripped out of a fairy tale or fantasy movie. I was waiting for one of the horses to say hello to me, or the coachman to break out in song about not wanting to be late, or some other nonsense. To my disappointment, they were perfectly ordinary, in their grand extraordinary way.

There were ice sculptures in another area. I assumed there was a competition, as a few of them had huge pretty ribbons next to them. I can't remember all the sculptures, but I remember focusing on one of them. Someone had sculpted a castle. I could have sworn it looked so similar, if not identical to the castle I had visited months prior.

I walked around to discover the many other activities the carnival had to offer. There was a huge outdoor ice rink, with fun music playing while you skated. Snowshoe rentals, a snowman building competition, tubing and tobogganing, and to my surprise a huge Ferris wheel that overlooked the winter wonderland. There were probably more, but that is what I saw, or at least, can remember.

There was a section for shopping as well. A lot of vendors sold what you would expect to see at an outdoor festival. A lot of weather-related items such as hats, mittens, gloves, and scarves. Some shops sold t-shirts and snow globes and other touristy stuff to remind you that you were there. Winter equipment was sold at a few other shops, along with jerseys from different sports clubs. I tried to see if I could find some of Dad's favourite teams but I didn't recognize any of the symbols or colour combinations. The toy shops were my favourites. There were gorgeous dolls I would have loved to have had a chance to play with. By that time, Lotus said we were getting too old for dolls, so I had to keep my admiration for them to myself. There were also about half a dozen jewellery stands with cheap and not-so-cheap pieces for sale. I saw a few pieces that would look great on Mom and Lotus, and a few necklaces I would consider wearing too.

Besides the activities, food and shopping, everything just looked so elegant and charming. The powdery white snow gave the carnival a beautiful foundation to build on. There were outdoor heaters scattered everywhere to escape the cold. Old-fashioned lamp posts decorated with ribbons and greenery surrounded each area. Trees had ribbons and lights strung in them. Lanterns were strung overhead. It was a shame that I had not come here at night. I can only imagine what everything would look like lit up by the lights and lanterns glowing. I was hoping to find out, but it wasn't meant to be.

I had noticed the tobogganing and tubing were free, and that the other kids were left to play on their own while their parents watched from the bottom of the hill. I figured this was a good place to start my carnival adventure, as I would not be asked about the whereabouts of my parents. There was a pile of tubes and different types of toboggans and sleds at the bottom of the hill. I grabbed a tube and started my ascent up the steep hill. It felt like it took forever to make my way to the top, but I made it. I found a good spot to place my tube and managed to get on it before it had the chance to go down the hill without me. I decided to go down the hill sitting up, with my legs crisscrossed. My first run would be a test to see how fast the hill is, and how brave I was feeling. I scooted to the edge, ready to claim my reward for the long uphill climb. As I pushed off, I started to feel what was becoming a familiar symptom. Nausea and dizziness took over, and before I could enjoy my ride I was gone.

I didn't expect to return to the restaurant. I guessed that I had spent two, maybe three hours at the carnival. That was a bit longer than my castle party adventure. With the experience from my first trip, I had already begun to believe that when I was gone, time did not stand still at home and that I wouldn't necessarily return to the place where I left, and my assumptions were right. When I opened my eyes I was home, in my bed. I felt tired and groggy, and it took a few seconds to properly sit up. It was obvious to me that while I was slowly coming to, that travelling was going to be hard on the body. My snowsuit was gone, and I was wearing the same clothes that I was wearing at the restaurant.

Mom must have heard me come back because she was in my room seconds after I returned. (To this day, she will not entertain my questions about what it sounds like when I do return. She has a really hard time about the whole thing.) She flew from the doorway to my bed, scooping me up in her arms and held me in a tight embrace. She yelled to Dad to let him know I was back, and he too leapt from the doorway to the bed, joining my mom, adding to the already too-tight welcome hug. I told Dad where I had been, explaining in detail the winter carnival I was just touring. I explained to him that I believed I was, without question, in a parallel universe because I did not recognize one sports team on any of the jerseys for sale. He listened intently, smiled and nodded as I told my story. It would take my Mom another three days to let me tell her about my recent trip.

That summer, my winter carnival adventure was the only time I travelled on my own. It was the only time I travelled at all. My parents cancelled our Bahamas cruise for what they called a "staycation." I overheard my parents fighting one night after they thought I had gone to sleep. Mom wanted to stay in the city, close to the hospital in case any complications emerged from my independent travelling. I felt fine.

School started in the fall without incident. Again, I was warned by my parents not to bring up anything about my first episode that happened at school last year or to talk about my travelling at all. Of course, I told Lotus everything. She had gone away with her family all summer, so school was the first time I had seen her in months.

Grade five was a bad year. I travelled in November, January, March and May. I am not going to go into detail about each excursion because I simply can't remember them all. I could even be off about the exact months, but I do know I left four times that school year. I wish I started to journal about these trips as they happened. (Yes Mom, you were right.) I have been going on my solo adventures for so long that I have started to lose track of where I have been and for how long. I can tell you that I remember that the duration of these trips was not long like my first two, which is probably why the details of my first two trips have remained so clear in my mind after all these years.

CHANGES

My parents argued a lot in my fifth-grade year. I could tell Mom was upset almost daily, but she tried to hide this from me. Dad just seemed stressed, constantly rubbing his face, or rubbing his fingers through his hair. During this time, my parents started to have a lot of meetings with lawyers, a lot of healthcare professionals, and various other people who I was left in the dark about. Long story short, when school was finished that year, there were a lot of changes put into place.

Mom sold her portion of her partnership with her law firm and was taking an extended break from practising law. Dad gave his notice at the hospital and bought a private practice in a small town an hour or so north of the city. Soon after, we bought a house just on the outskirts of that small town. They moved me away from my friends, my school, and my life. I had known nothing but the city, our house, our street, and our friends. The most devastating part of all this was saying goodbye to Mrs. McKenzie. Mom said that moving forward, she would be home every day with me, so my beloved nanny was not needed anymore. To me, she wasn't just "hired help," she was part of the family, and I loved her.

There were so many drastic changes, all at once, and they were all because of me. I begged my parents to reverse their decisions. I promised not to leave anymore, but my parents and I knew that was a hollow promise. I had no control over this. They sat me down and explained their reasoning behind ruining my life.

The first decision was to pull me out of school. I missed a lot that year. My parents kept me home for weeks at a time after each journey. It felt like I was home more than not. They decided that enrolling me in school next year would be a waste of time if I kept missing so much of it. It was decided that I would be homeschooled for the foreseeable future.

Instead of hiring a tutor or full-time homeschooling teacher, Mom decided she wanted to stay home and take care of my education. She explained that since I started travelling, she has not been able to focus on her work and was afraid of losing cases and clients. She thought it best for her clients, her law firm, and her reputation if she stepped away for now.

Dad bought the private practice to be home more. He would have regular working hours and would be home most evenings and weekends. Last summer they didn't want to travel so that we would be close to the hospital, fearing complications from my trips, so I was surprised that they planned to move us just over an hour away from any decent hospital. There is a hospital about a half-hour's drive from where we now live, but my dad is a bit of a hospital snob. He was one of the top surgeons in the city, so I guess he has a right to be. He had agreed when he left his previous place of work, that he would give them two days a month for complicated, specialty surgeries, and would come for surgical emergencies if there were no other options. Besides that, he was going to work a nine-to-five job for the first time in his life.

So why did my dad not just open a private practice in the city? Why did he find it necessary to move us to practically country living? The goal was to reduce stress. It was explained to me, that it was suggested to my parents, that the city may start to feel overwhelming upon my return, especially as I have been leaving more often. This seemed like nonsense to me, as the city's hustle and bustle is all I have ever known. It was also suggested that perhaps a more calming environment might act as a sort of preventative measure to keep me from travelling. Spoiler alert, it didn't.

We moved, and I was miserable.

THE NEW HOUSE

I secretly loved our new house right away. I had to love it in secret out of protest for ripping me away from everything I had ever known, and everyone I ever loved. We had a three-story townhouse in the city. I had the biggest house out of all my friends. We were a successful family, with a house to match. Each room was carefully designed by some overpriced interior designer. It was open concept, modern, and comfortable. When I was told we were moving to just a two-story house, I was instantly disappointed in the downgrade. I didn't want to hear any more about it. After Mrs. McKenzie's last day with me, I tried to shut myself off from everyone the last week in the city. I spent every last minute I could in my old room, being forced out for meals and bathroom breaks. I didn't want to hear about the new house, the new town, or want any part of this new exciting life I kept being told we were going to have. I loved my room dearly. It was a purple paradise, redesigned by myself after my purple party. I didn't want to let it go, but the day quickly came when I had to. The movers showed up and unless I wanted to be packed into a box, I had to surrender my hold on the room.

We spent the last two nights in the city in a hotel suite while our stuff was packed and moved. My parents tried to improve my mood through bribery, taking me shopping and buying me my favourite treats. It was working until the morning of the move snuck up on me.

The new house is big, huge, grand, no, ginormous compared to our townhouse. My parents bought a five-bedroom, two-story house, with a walkout basement. Four bedrooms make up the second story of the house. The sizes of the rooms still blow my mind to this day. My room is larger than my parent's master bedroom in the townhouse. The main floor has a den, a living room, a dining room, a second sitting room, and an eat-in kitchen that is quadrupled the size of our last. The basement has a huge open space for entertaining and TV viewing, an office, and a fifth bedroom that has been turned into a gym. The house sits on two acres of land. I remember feeling worried about getting lost on my own property. We didn't have a yard in the city. You would walk to parks if you wanted to see and enjoy some greenery. Not only do we have massive green lawns, trees and gardens, but we also have a pond near the back. To me, it looks like something you would rent if you wanted the perfect country holiday.

The town we live in isn't even a real town. We now live in a hamlet, in between two villages, which are even smaller than a town. Dad joked that we lived in a ham sandwich. I remember rolling my eyes, and telling him he was lame, but secretly thought that was hilarious, and used that joke later when I chatted with Lotus. I wasn't ready to be happy and laugh at Dad's jokes yet, I was still in full protest mode. We didn't even live in the hamlet.

We were on the outskirts. It was peaceful but suffocating at the same time. We could go days, even weeks without seeing anyone if we had enough groceries and supplies. During the first few months in the new house, I would hide snacks and drinks so we would have to make extra trips into town. Mom caught on pretty quickly to what I was doing. She saw my need for interaction and people-watching. She started taking me into the villages regularly to just walk around, to see people, and to be seen.

The main village we always shop at has a little grocery store, post office, bank, different little clothing and jewellery shops, a few mom-and-pop type restaurants and coffee shops, one gas station, and a few other businesses. It also has a police and fire station, which is nice. It has one elementary school. High school students are bussed to a neighbouring town. My dad's office is not in the village but in a larger town about a fifteen-minute drive from us. We relied on the shops for a few supplies but once every week or so we went out of town to get most of our groceries and goods from the major stores.

NOW

Everything changed drastically, fast, and all at once. My parents promised me that we would find a way to keep me connected with my friends. Since I was to be homeschooled, I wouldn't be making any new friends, so I held my parents to that promise. I saw Lotus and a few other girls in our group roughly every other weekend. Their parents would drive them to my house for a sleepover, or my mom would take me to one of their houses. Mom would stay in a nearby hotel, always fearful I would leave. This worked out great for the first year and a bit, but as we got older, groups and friendship dynamics changed. From then on, it has just been me and Lotus.

As we have gotten older, every other weekend, became once a month, and sometimes longer. Lotus thrived as she got older. She became quite popular with the girls and boys. She was on various sports teams and was involved in student council. I didn't want to hold her social life back, so I saw her when her schedule allowed. As I got older I started to travel a lot more and for longer periods at a time, so that got in the way too. Thank goodness for technology. We video-called a lot and texted almost daily. She has made good friends at school, but there was something about our honest friendship that we both needed and cherished. She was also the only person who I could honestly talk to about my trips. My parents decided after our move, to be open-minded about my travels and wanted to hear details, but I could tell they were just humouring me on some level. I can't explain it. With Lotus, there was no judgment. I could tell her how I truly felt, and explain little details like if there were any cute guys, or confess how I even missed my home, and parents, while I was away. In return, she could bitch freely about her friends, who she was dating, teachers, her parents, or anything else judgement free. Present day, nothing has changed. We still try to make time to visit one another, and she texts me all the time with her fun and envious dilemmas. She is currently in a love triangle, dating a guy and a girl, trying to figure out what to do. Each partner believes they are the only one she is dating. I'm still the only one who will give her advice she doesn't want to hear. (She is going to kill me if she ever reads this.)

Dad's private practice is still thriving. He is the only doctor in town. He has stopped his twice-monthly visits to the city for specialty appointments. He tells me he is too busy for that now, but I know he doesn't want to be far from home because of me. He lives a slower pace of life now, but I feel he has aged faster than most men his age. He still runs most mornings but doesn't exercise to the extent that he used to. His hair is now a salt and pepper mixture, compared to the perfect black gloss it used to be. I'm told he is still super attractive, (like all the time, ew) by anyone we meet, but even I can see his looks are now just an echo of what he once was, or even could potentially still be. To me, he just looks tired and worried all the time, but would never admit feeling like that to me.

The same could be said about Mom. She has also seemed to have aged beyond the six years we have been in this house, despite our calm, laid-back way of life. She has developed so many worry lines. Her hair is still neat, but greying. She is still stylish and classy but has traded in her designer suits for practical slacks, blouses and flowing dresses.

I worried about Mom when we first moved, and I still worry about her now. Her career was everything to her. There was never a time in her life when she wasn't busting her butt working. She kept reassuring me and still assures me that she is happy and feels fulfilled but I know she is just presenting a strong front. She won't admit it, but I know she feels lost. In addition to being responsible for educating me, she has had various hobbies over the years that have come and gone. She would get obsessively excited about each one until a new obsession took over. She self-taught herself how to knit and was sure she was going to make it a side business. (She continues to knit hats for newborns for the nearest hospital.) After a few hats, scarves and a blanket, she moved on to pottery, self-taught of course. After we ran out of room for her many jars and vases, she moved on to furniture revival. I swear she painted or re-stained every single piece of furniture in our house. Jewellery making, gardening, sewing, painting, making jam, and butter, a very brief introduction into woodworking, guitar, piano and even bird watching are the hobbies that I can remember her attempting. I can only conclude that she has been trying to fill some sort of empty feeling. Trying to feel accomplished again.

I recently overheard her talking on the phone to her old law firm. They have been trying to convince her for years to do some sort of consulting work for them, that she can do without ever leaving the house. I hope she finally accepts their offer. Work would bring a bit of joy back into her life.

My parents still have a great relationship, but even I can see that it feels a bit strained. They never go on dates anymore or do anything for themselves. Their focus is always on me. To me, this doesn't make sense. I don't know how many times I have tried to explain to them how they are free to enjoy time together when I am gone on my adventures. But statements like that usually leave my mom bursting into tears and my dad needing to quietly fix something in the garage.

Then there is me. Hey! Did I mention my name yet? Should I have done this at the beginning? See, no clue what I am doing.

My name is Elizabeth. I know, a very common, not cool, ordinary name. I think sixty percent of the girls I know have it as their middle name. Mom thought it was classic and timeless. I didn't care for it. When I was young, I made everyone call me Lizard, and would only respond to that name. Dad still calls me that once in a while, but only he can. Mom uses my entire proper name. Lotus calls me Lizy or Liz.

I haven't changed too much. I am still blonde, but now a deeper golden compared to the bright golden blonde I was as a child. I just keep it long and natural.

I still have the whisky-coloured brown eyes, that for some reason people kind of go crazy over. One time a cashier wouldn't stop comparing my eyes to the eyes of the vampire family in the movie Twilight. You know, the vegetarians who only drink animal blood. It must have been the way the terrible fluorescent lighting was hitting my eyes because I don't think they look similar at all. I swear my mom started loading the groceries on the belt slower to prolong the awkward exchange.

I am tall but only made it to five-foot-seven and a half. Yes, that half matters. I have no idea how I didn't end up any taller, with the parents I have. It is truly one of life's great mysteries.

I dress pretty normally. I am a jeans, t-shirt and sweater kind of girl. I am currently seventeen years old and Mom is still trying to put a skirt or dress on me. When I am home, which is most of the time, I am lounging in workout clothes. When I am not travelling, my mom has me glued to a computer (and now this old-school journal) to catch up on my schooling.

Because my social life is pretty non-existent, I keep my makeup very minimal. I love jewellery but I don't wear a lot of that either. I have a drugstore thumb ring that never comes off, and I wear the same studded earrings every day. I have a jewellery box full of really nice expensive pieces that my parents keep gifting me. I hope one day I have an excuse to wear some of it. My parents need to let me out of the house first.

EARLY TRIPS

I feel I'm getting sidetracked. The task I was given was to journal about my travels and experiences. I guess, if someone were to actually read this, I would want you to know some of the back story, of how I came to travel, and how I have come to my current situation. I think, or I hope that I did a decent job with that. Before I start to keep accounts of my most recent travels and catch you up to the present, I will do my best to quickly recap the trips that I remember.

As I have mentioned before, I can't remember the exact timelines of all my travels or keep straight in my mind where or when I have been and for how long. I was only a young kid when I started travelling. Writing details down when I came back each time seemed like a logical thing to do, but it just didn't happen. I'll admit that I'm glad that I am being "highly encouraged" to do this now. It will be interesting to see how many journals I will be able to fill with accounts of all my adventures. I may have quite the collection someday.

As I reflect back on my trips, I have realized that my experiences have shifted as I got older. You could say, that each trip was age-appropriate. In my early days,

I visited some pretty cool, beautiful picturesque places. I just remember feeling a sense of calmness, joy and an overwhelming feeling of belonging. It was as if I was purposely put in places or simple situations where I could just enjoy the uncomplicated scenery. In the first few years, I was always dropped into parties and festivals, with a lot of kids my age running around, much like my castle and winter carnival adventure.

Here are some highlights of my favourite destinations, the places that have stuck with me.

A paper lantern festival. Hundreds of lanterns were lit and released into the sky over a lake.

A huge community picnic, where there were hundreds of families on hundreds of blankets, with hundreds of picnic baskets. I remember the live music, the smell of freshly baked goods, and the laughter.

A petting zoo was fun. I spent hours being attacked by the most adorable, affectionate baby goats. I only really remember the goats and the intense earthy smells. Poop. I smelled a lot of poop.

There was a magic show where I was fortunate enough to sit in the front row. When you are a kid, magic shows seem so real, but I have a feeling that I witnessed real magic that day. Those of us in the audience saw the magician take a chicken and transform it into a cat right in front of our eyes without smoke, curtains or mirrors. What else could it be besides real magic?

The hot air balloon rides were cool. I was too chicken to get in one, but it was still so fun to watch them slowly rise into the air. There were so many, and each balloon was unique and colourful.

I found myself observing a lot of contests. Pie eating, hotdog eating, well, there were a lot of eating contests. Photography, fashion design, painting, carving, cooking and baking. My favourite was the talent shows. They mostly involved singing, which I loved, even though I didn't recognize any of the songs.

I was brought to a lot of natural touristy landscapes. A lot of cliffs, caves, and waterfalls. They were pretty to see, but after a few minutes, those trips became boring.

The aquarium adventure was something else. It was the first trip that had a real effect on me and made an impact on my normal life back home. I remember being in one of those clear plastic bubbles where the sea life swam around you, only this didn't make me feel sad like the other aquariums I had gone to with my parents. It felt as if we were dropped in the middle of the ocean, and it wasn't the sharks and fish that were in a tank, but we were. We observed these beautiful creatures in their natural habitat, instead of ripping them away from their proper bodies of water and imprisoning them in an unnatural small tank. Wherever I was, I just felt in my heart that this place got it right. I remember I had tears in my eyes as I watched the aquatic scene all around me. When I got back, I had the idea in my head that I was going to be a marine biologist, or whatever I had to become, to recreate what I saw. I was going to save all sea life. That lasted for about two years. I'm sure I drove my parents crazy. I refused to eat any seafood, but I was ok with other sources of meat. My parents laugh about this now, and so do I, but I'm sure it was a long two years for them.

DARK TIMES

The first few years were simple. I travelled, watched the shows, sometimes got to play, I had fun, enjoyed the scenery, and then went home after a few hours. When I was fourteen, about year five into my travels, I went through what I call, my dark phase. I was starting to leave more often and for longer periods of time. The length of my trips started to not coincide with time back home like it used to. Before, if I were gone for three hours, only three hours would pass at home. I could literally leave after lunch, go on some whirlwind adventure, and be back in time for family dinner. I'm not saying it always worked out like that, I travelled at sporadic times, but it made life bearable for my family and friends. Now, what felt like a couple of hours for me, would be half a day at home, or longer. I started missing play dates with Lotus, including her birthday. My parents had to cancel appointments and outings because I was gone. My parents just seemed sad all the time. I started falling behind in my schoolwork, and I became confused as to what the date was or even what day of the week we were on. I felt like I was spiralling out of control.

At first, I use to feel that my travelling was this

unique power, gifted to me, but for the first time, it felt more like a burden. I hated it. I hated what it was doing to everyone I loved and I hated myself. When I did leave during this time, I would spend my time away in a quiet corner, where I would close my eyes, put my hands over my ears and wait out the time, willing myself to go back home. How could I enjoy myself when I was causing so much trouble and sadness back home? I couldn't tell you where I went for months, because I refused to participate. There could have been a park with real-life freakin' dinosaurs in front of me and I wouldn't have known or cared. When I was home I was quiet, moody, and difficult. I pushed away anyone close to me, so I couldn't hurt them. Lotus was disappointed I missed her birthday, but I think she would have understood if I had just talked to her. Instead, I pushed her away too. I stopped talking to her for almost a year. I felt lonely, and I made sure to remain that way as a means to punish myself, for something I had no control over.

CAMI

I t wasn't until I turned fifteen that people started to talk to me while on my adventures. I will never forget the first time it happened. I was still in my doom and gloom phase. I had travelled to somewhere crowded and loud. I desperately searched for a quiet spot to hide as I waited to leave, but there were no quiet places or secluded spots. I was in an open field, the sun was setting, and there were huge lights all around illuminating the area. There were hundreds of people in every direction I looked. There was nowhere to hide. I was tempted to just fall to the ground where I stood, hug myself into the fetal position, and just wait out the time, but I was afraid of getting trampled, or worse, drawing attention to myself. Panic had started to set in. Besides the very first time I travelled, up until now, I had never felt any negative emotions on a trip, at least, not like this. Breathing became difficult as if the air had become thick, and it was hard to draw enough air into my lungs to satisfy a proper breath. It felt like everyone around me was moving faster than they should be able to, the talking and laughter got louder, the lights got brighter, and my head started to go numb. I started to have tunnel vision, and right before

I was about to lose all control and possibly faint, I felt someone grab my arms, and a girl's voice asked "Are you ok?"

At first, I just saw pink. Was a pink orb talking to me? Had I finally lost it? The voice repeated the question, and as I felt a hand on each arm squeezing gently, I found myself becoming more grounded and was able to focus. As my eyes started to adjust, and the opening of the black tunnels started to get bigger, I saw a girl on the other side of the outreached arms, keeping me up. She was around my age, give or take a year or two, and had bright pink hair. She was wearing a lot of makeup, but not enough to hide the kindness in her eyes.

"I'm ok, I think I was having a panic attack." I heard my voice answer back.

"Are you here alone?"

"Yes." I felt like I was someone else watching this exchange. It was strange to hear my voice. It was strange to even talk to someone.

"Cool, me too. My name is Cami, want to watch together?" She had asked excitedly.

Watch? I took a deep breath and finally allowed myself to look properly at my surroundings. Behind Cami, in the distance, there was a huge stage where loud music was being produced. I was at a music festival.

"Yeah, that would be great," I finally answered.

"This band sucks, but they are almost finished. Let's go find a good spot for the next band." As Cami said this, she linked her arm with mine, and we started walking in the direction of the stage. She was right, as soon as we got close, the band who were just playing were starting to leave the stage. We were able to find a good spot, standing somewhat close to the stage. Cami warned me that if we went any closer we would probably get trampled by crazy people.

While we waited for the music to start, I took the time to study Cami and the other concertgoers. It was a weird scene. The clothing had a 1980s vibe. Old-school Madonna meets London's 1980s punk scene. Leather, plaid, and band shirts were paired with lace, pearls and other oversized jewellery, denim, short skirts and even some tutu-looking things. Cami's Bright pink hair was big and loud. Her makeup matched with her loud purple lipstick, heavy blush, thick eyeliner and pink eye shadows. She wore a strategically ripped t-shirt, with what I assumed was a band's logo. She wore a poofy tulle-like, underskirt type thing as her skirt with fishnet stockings and huge chunky black boots. She had on leather armbands that went from her hands to almost her elbows, coupled with bracelets and bangles. She had her nose and tongue pierced, which I thought was so cool as she was so young. It took me years before I was allowed to get a set of second holes in my ear lobes, so I knew face piercings would never be an option for me as long as I lived at home.

After I finished studying everyone, I finally took a good look at my ensemble. I was wearing what looked like Chuck Taylor's (there was a logo I didn't recognize), black, which laced up to a few inches under my knee. I had on a red and black plaid and leather skirt. I too wore a faded black band shirt, with a logo I didn't know. Mine wasn't ripped, and fit properly, if not a bit tight. I had black fishnet arm sleeves on both arms. They looped around my middle finger and went to my elbow. I had on three long, chunky necklaces, each a different length. A black leather bracelet with spikes decorated one wrist, and silver bangles on the other. I loved every piece and I felt so cool. I did not have access to a mirror, so I am not sure if my makeup matched everyone's or if I was even wearing any. My hair was a mystery to me as well.

Cami made small talk about the upcoming band as we waited for them to get on stage. She wanted to know if I had seen them before and told me random facts about them. When the band finally came on stage, the small talk ended and we focused on the music. It was rock, meets 1980s pop, meets punk, meets techno. I thought it was pretty cool and I let the music and energy of the crowd consume me. Cami's warning about getting too close to the stage was warranted. There was an extremely energetic mosh pit at the foot of the stage, whether they called it a mosh pit as we did back home, I have no idea. Cami and I jumped and danced for the duration of the band's set which lasted about an hour. It had been months since I allowed myself to feel any resemblance of joy, so this was freeing if not medicinal.

When the show ended, I was surprised I hadn't left yet. I normally make my departure after a few hours. Cami linked our arms again and we were on the hunt for the food trucks. We settled on a truck that served burgers and fries, gathered our food and found a spot on the ground to sit that wasn't polluted with people. I know we chatted about typical teenager stuff, like boyfriends or in my case, lack thereof, clothes, and music, but I can't remember specifics. That is until we got to the topic of best friends. When Cami asked me about my best friend,

I broke down and poured my heart out to this girl I barely knew as if she were a therapist. I tried to explain the situation without having to explain my strange way of travelling as best as I could. Cami listened to my tear-soaked rambles. When I was done explaining the situation, Cami convinced me that it wasn't too late to reach out. She explained that if Lotus was a true friend, she would come back if I opened myself up to her again. Spending time with Cami showed me what I have been missing in my life. My life has become so chaotic and unpredictable, and I am missing out on a lot at home, but pushing the few relationships I have away has become unhealthy. If anything, I need emotional support now more than ever.

I ended up spending the entire night at this music festival. Cami and I watched four or five more bands. We danced and acted silly together until the sun started to come up. That was when Cami had to say goodbye and go home. If you are thinking it strange that a teenage girl was at an all-night rock music festival on her own, you are not alone. This came to mind throughout the entire night I was with her and had meant to ask her about it, but it was like something was blocking me from asking her that question. It would be on the tip of my tongue and then something would distract us both from the conversation. Then I had just forgotten about asking altogether. It wasn't until she left that all my questions and concerns came flooding back. It was the strangest feeling and didn't make sense, but neither did my travelling, so I just accepted that maybe this was normal here, or it just wasn't my business and chose to let it go.

When I watched her walk away, the familiar

nauseated dizzy feeling took over and I returned home.

My parents were waiting for me when I got back. I was at the music festival for approximately ten hours. That equated to three days here. Three days! That was the longest I had been away from home. When I recovered from the weakness I got from travelling, I told my parents where I had been and the significance of the trip. I told them about Cami. Cami will forever have a place in my heart. Thanks to my very brief friendship with her, over time, I was able to weasel my way back into Lotus's life again. I mended our friendship and I worked out some stuff with my parents as well. I learned that they needed me as much as I needed their support. I'm not saying everything was perfect from then on, but once again, we had more of an open dialogue.

Cami and the festival also inspired me to dig through Dad's record collection. I stole all his old punk records and CDs, and anything he had that you can't hear on the radio. I went through a heavy eyeliner, black clothing, alternative phase for almost two years. Dad thought it was great and we bonded further over it. Mom went with it but I know she secretly hated it and confirmed my suspicion recently when I found her doing a happy dance when I started to introduce colour back into my wardrobe. I still listen to the music, but I found a more subtle style that is more me, to Mom's relief.

SCHOOL DANCE

A part of me is beginning to believe that on a subconscious level, my brain, which I assume is responsible for my gift, was (and currently is) sending me to experiences that I have not yet experienced. Experiences and situations that a normal teenager would take for granted. Experiences I was so desperate to have for myself.

A few weeks before the trip I am about to describe, Lotus and I were talking about her upcoming winter formal dance. Mom had driven me into the city so I could spend a couple of days at Lotus's house, on condition that we didn't go anywhere. Mom stayed in a nearby hotel like usual. Lotus and I spent most of the weekend in her room, where we worked together trying to choose the perfect dress, out of the many she had purchased, to wear to the formal.

I have never been to a school dance. I have never danced with a boy. I desperately wanted to go to one. I want to wear a dress that I would think is cool now, but I will probably laugh about it in twenty years. Have a date that my dad would completely scare the crap out of, and then threaten him about my curfew as we were leaving. I want to wear a corny corsage on my wrist. I just want to be around others my age and have carefree fun.

Lotus and I begged my parents to let me accompany her to the upcoming dance. Her girlfriend at the time was even cool with me going as her plus one. We even suggested that *both* my parents could chaperone, even though that would be completely embarrassing and lame, but we were desperate. My parents were afraid that the dance would be overly stimulating for me and trigger an untimely departure. Technically, all my departures were untimely, but they wouldn't hear that argument. As a consolation prize, I was given two nights with Lotus, in the city, but under house arrest.

I had fun helping Lotus prepare for her dance. We decided on a long dark green dress, with spaghetti straps, and a slit in the side. She was going to look amazing. During those two days, we tried on some dresses, took too many selfies, ate too much junk food, talked about her love life, which always seemed complicated, and watched our favourite movies.

"Next year, we will try again next year," Lotus said as I was gathering my stuff to leave. "You will be seventeen next year, so maybe they won't hold on to you so tightly. I'll find you a date, and we will have a blast!" As she said it, I could tell that *she* didn't even believe that would be possible. She could never hide how she feels. Her facial expressions always gave her away.

She was right, of course. The answer was a solid no again this year.

Three weeks after that weekend, I travelled.

I arrived inside a school, where I could hear a lot of loud noises and louder music. It took me very little time to realize I was at a school dance! I wanted to laugh and cry, from the overwhelming emotions I felt.

When I arrived, I was standing just outside the school's gym entrance. Luckily I arrived when no one else was standing in this area, so no one saw me appear out of thin air. Thinking back, I am not sure anyone has ever seen me arrive during any of my trips. Or at least if they had, no one has ever made a big deal about it.

I was taken to a place where technology looked superior to what we have now, yet music and fashion had only evolved to what we would know as the 1970s here. I mean, at least I assume what the 1970s could have looked like, at least from what I have seen from shows and movies. Or maybe the 1990s? You know how fashion keeps coming back, or so I'm told, by Mom, constantly. Every time I go shopping she keeps telling me all the stuff I'm picking out, (or what she keeps trying to pick out for me) she wore in the 1990s. Insert eye roll emoji. But the makeup, hair, and clothes heavily suggested a 1970s vibe to me.

Immediately I looked to see what I was wearing. I had on a light blue dress. It was long and flowy, hugged me at the waist, and had a v-neck neckline and big flowy sleeves that were cuffed right before my elbow. It wouldn't be what I, or probably anyone in this century, would pick, but it was still pretty and I felt pretty in it. My hair was down and curled in the front. I remember thinking that I needed to find a mirror, so I could get a proper look at myself to take a mental picture and find out if I had blue eyeshadow on. These are details Lotus would want to know.

The gym was decorated with streamers and balloons. There were a ridiculous amount of streamers, mostly hung from the ceiling. Each streamer started heavily taped in the middle of the room and branched off, twisted and tapped, hanging above the heads of the dancers. In the middle of the streamers hung a disco ball. I guess those are universal everywhere. I remember laughing when I saw it. Balloons were scattered about everywhere. It didn't look like there was a decorative plan as to where they should be. The colour scheme must have been "all the colours" and I'm guessing the budget was small, but to me, it was perfect. Everyone should get the opportunity to attend a low-budget school dance at least once in their life.

This sounds silly, but my first thought was to see if there was a punch bowl. In TV shows and movies, there is always a punch bowl, and someone's date is always sent off to get them a glass of punch. When I finally stepped inside the gym, it didn't take me long to find the tables where snacks and beverages were laid out. As I approached the table, I had the hardest time containing my excitement and keeping it cool, because, in the centre of the snack table, there was a huge clear glass punch bowl, surrounded by matching punch bowl little cups. The punch itself was red, and it even had floating citrus fruit on top. It was a dream come true. The only thing that could have made this moment better, is if someone had spiked the punch.

(Ok, Mom, Dad, just chill. I know what you are thinking, but I was sixteen and it was normal for people my age to want to try, or have already partaken in alcohol. As much as you treat me like a caged, fragile animal, Lotus and I have stolen a bottle of champagne or wine on many occasions. So there. What are you going to do? Ground me? I'm already practically grounded forever.)

The punch was not spiked, but I thoroughly

enjoyed the fruity mixture just the same.

I stepped off to the side, so as not to be in the way of my fellow punch drinkers. I remember feeling so happy. There could be better, fancier words to describe that moment, but I like "happy." I stood there, sipping the best punch I have ever had, swaying to the music I have never heard before, people watching and just enjoying the atmosphere.

"This is enough" I remember saying to myself. If my internal navigator decided to leave at that moment, I wouldn't have been mad about it. My heart already felt so full.

That is when I noticed this ridiculously good-looking guy walking toward me. He was tall, with bleach-blonde hair and intense blue eyes. He had on a very faint blue dress shirt, that was frilly around the buttons down the shirt. The shirt was slightly too small, but not in a bad way. It was clear he played some kind of sport. His biceps were begging to be set free. His dress pants were dark brown, with a slight flare at the bottom, and brown dress shoes finished his look.

At first, I assumed he was heading for the punch, but it soon became clear that he was walking a determined path that didn't lead to anything or anyone else. If my heart was already full, it was about to panic, burst, and maybe throw up a little bit in my mouth.

He talked to me, and I managed to talk back. Do I remember what was said? NOPE! Do you know that feeling when you are super nervous, excited and scared all at the same time? Your vision goes a bit fuzzy, your head starts to get warmer by the minute and your hearing keeps going in and out. That is all I remember about that exchange. I couldn't have been a total spaz though, because he asked me to dance and I managed to say yes.

He took my hand (holy shit, first time holding hands with a boy!) and led me to the dance floor, while my brain was screaming 'HOLY SHIT! First slow dance with a boy!'

We arrived on the dance floor, accompanied by a dozen or so more couples. As if on cue, the lights dimmed, and a soft, slow song started to play. He respectfully put his hands on my hips, and I put my hands on his shoulders. He gave me this cute smirk, and then we started to slowly dance.

It was a perfect moment. When I think back to it, I can still smell his cologne, something sandalwood-like, feel his warm hands on my hips, and smell his breath, a mixture of mint and punch. (Listen, I'll never get over the punch, so deal with it.) I can still feel the warm, slightly stuffy air. In my head, I heard the song "Crimson and Clover" as we danced, but I honestly don't think that song exists in whatever version of Earth I was visiting.

The song was maybe a quarter of the way through, and I was enjoying this most perfect moment when I felt this odd, almost tingling sensation like I was being watched. I looked up and noticed a guy watching me, who was dancing a few couples away from me. Immediately I thought it was completely inappropriate as we both had dancing partners, to which our attention should be focused. I gave him my best "what are you looking at, you are kind of being a jerk, pay attention to the pretty girl in your arms" look before my partner spun me around out of view. I swear I saw him smile before I turned away.

Inevitably, my partner made his way slowly around, through the imaginary circle all couples were following in their respective space on the dancefloor, which brought me right back into the weird guy's view. This time, I was prepared to give him a more severe scowling look. When I glanced over, I was taken aback to find that he and his partner had made their way closer to us. They managed to move right beside us. This time, as his eyes once again found mine, they had this hauntingly knowing look in them, accompanied by a slight smile. It was as if he were seeing right through me and knew all my deep and darkest secrets. It was so unnerving. I gasped, stumbled, and stepped on my partner's foot. I heard him giggle as I profusely apologized to my partner, and let him lead me once again around our slow circle. When Rude Boy (that is his name now) came back into view, I snuck another look, and then I really looked at him. He was tall, had nice clothes, (nothing too frilly anyway), had dark, wavy hair and was annoyingly attractive. He caught me studying him, and our eyes locked once again. His eyes were so dark, you could almost mistake them for black. There was something impossibly familiar about them.

It couldn't be.

I had an instant flashback to the Regency Era party I ended up crashing on my first trip. There is no way he could be the same boy, who kept choosing me to play with all those years ago.

By this time, I had concluded that I travelled to parallel universes. That is the only explanation for every place I have been to. Each place I visit is a version of our Earth, but in its own place in time, and each is different from the next. So by that logic, this could not be the same boy. And surely, the same pair of eyes could be found on hundreds, if not thousands of different boys' faces in this universe alone.

But my body would not listen to logic. I suddenly had a hard time breathing, and the room felt like it had started to spin. I assumed I was getting ready to leave this place and return home. As I was trying to catch my breath, I saw Rude Boy come towards me to try to help, but my dance partner beat him to my aid. He sat me down, gave me some water and talked to me while my panic attack became manageable. When I felt like I could function on my own, I released my partner, so he could dance with other girls, which left me free to pursue this matter with Rude Boy.

I had to talk to him. I just had to know. As I searched for him near the beverage and treat tables, among the dancing bodies, in every dark corner, I was coming up with a plan on how to ask him what I needed to ask, without giving away who I was or what I could do. If he isn't the same boy, I didn't want to sound like a crazy person. Well, crazier than I already am anyway. I searched for him for what felt like an hour. While I searched the hallways of the school, I started to assume he had left the dance, so I was ready to give up. I convinced myself that I built up the entire thing in my mind. Maybe he thought I was cute, or maybe I had something on my face (I never did find a mirror), and this amused him while we were dancing, but that's it.

I quietly laughed out loud, shook my head to centre myself, and started to walk back to the dance. Rude Boy wasn't the only good-looking boy in the gym, and I started getting excited at the prospect of dancing with as many of them as I could. At this point, I still haven't had my first kiss, so I was thinking that could be a possibility too.

I started down the hallway in the direction of the

gym, walking with anticipation and purpose, the music becoming louder with each step I took.

I would never make it back to the dance.

When I turned the last corner, I was met with those impossibly deep dark eyes. Rude Boy was standing at the end of the hall, in front of the gym entrance. The feelings I had pushed aside and rationalized came flooding back, and I knew I just had to talk to him. I started towards him, walking with increased urgency. To my surprise, he was doing the same toward me. As we got closer I could swear I could see a look of anticipation on his face. My heart felt like it was going to burst out of my chest.

His look of anticipation quickly changed to concern and regret. At first, I couldn't understand why the sudden change, but then the familiar feeling of nausea and dizziness came over me. I was leaving.

Before I lost consciousness, I could have sworn I heard him yell "No!" That sound would haunt me for a long time.

When I returned home from my first school dance, I was met with frantic parents, like always. Mom fussed over me, and Dad gave me an extensive check-up. This has become the norm, so I have stopped fighting it. When my parents finally left me alone, I was able to call Lotus. I needed to tell her what happened, and in return, she needed all the details, no matter how small or insignificant. I always tell her about my trips, but this time it felt different, special. I finally experienced something a normal teenager would get to do. I didn't feel like I was talking about a whacky adventure, that only she believes I went on. It was a normal phone conversation about boys, clothes, music and dances.

Lotus and I talked about Rude Boy for the majority

of the call. I explained to her my theories about what could have happened.

Theory number one - I had crap on my face, so he was bullying me.

Theory number two - He thought I was attractive and was acting completely inappropriately.

Theory number three - He, inexplicably, is the same boy from my first ever trip, and we recognized each other.

I have tried to rationalize the experience, with the help of Lotus, and obsessed over it without her. Theories one and two are uncomplicated and normal. I desperately wanted either one of those to be the explanation, the truth, about what happened, but my gut was not cooperating. The first two theories can't explain the intense feeling I had when I looked into his weirdly familiar eyes, or when he yelled "no!" which I am certain I heard upon my departure. Lotus and I both agree something significant may have happened, and that I need to be careful. We don't know who he is, or what kind of person he is. Lotus thinks he could even be dangerous, but I didn't get that impression. The truth is, when I looked into his eyes, aside from the panic attack I had, that familiarity didn't feel remotely scary. It felt warm and inviting, like home.

POST-DANCE DRAMA

After the drama at the school dance, (I am still relishing in the fact that I was involved in drama at a school dance), all I could think about was Rude Boy. No, it wasn't a crush. I know you are thinking that, but it wasn't. Seriously! I was intrigued. He was a mystery that needed to be solved. Or he wasn't and I built the entire thing up in my mind. Mystery versus dumb boy. That is what was going through my brain twenty-four-seven.

Lotus's winter formal was in early December. My winter dance was in late February.

I travelled two more times before I turned my current age of seventeen. I am almost ashamed to talk about the trips because my behaviour was anything but cool.

I never really look forward to leaving. As I mentioned before, I struggled with how it affected everyone at home. I still struggle with it now. However, after my incident with Rude Boy, I found myself becoming impatient to leave again, which was terrible of me. I tried to deny it, but deep down, that was how I felt. I didn't dare share this with anyone, not even Lotus, but I guess they will find out one day if they ever read this.

It was about mid-March when nausea and dizziness washed over me. Within the hour, I was brought to what was the most beautiful library I had ever seen, in real life, or thanks to the internet. Picture floor-to-ceiling books, many stories high (I'm not a good judge of height or measurements, so bear with me), paired with ceilings comparable to the Sistine Chapel. It felt like they took a museum, already containing ancient relics, and filled it with books. There were statues and what looked like century-old paintings displayed throughout. Sadly, I can't begin to give this place the proper description it deserves, because about ten minutes after I arrived, my stupid teenage brain went into hormonal overdrive, and all I could think about was Rude Boy.

What are the chances he could be here? Is this even in the same universe as the dance? And if it was, would I even be in the same country? Does he even like to read? Could he be here on a school trip? Am I even in the same decade as that school dance? (Visitors' clothing suggested that was a no). What do I say if I do find him? Will he think I am stalking him? Do I have something on my face?

After I exhausted my brain with questions, I decided that I would just simply look for him, and worry later about what happens if I do find him.

I walked around for a couple of hours. This place was huge. I noticed that each room, or area, had a different theme, or expressed a different time period. My favourite was a gothic-like room. It was dark, with beautiful dark stained wood that was heavily used throughout, accompanied by beautiful archways. The lighting was dull, compared to other areas, and the artwork and statues felt very medieval. I suspected that books containing darker histories, or otherworldly topics could be found in this area. I regret not taking the time to actually check out a few of the books, but my mind was solely focused on the task I had given myself, the search for Rude Boy.

After hours of walking, I realized that if he were here and walking around, I might not find him by walking around too. I found an area with long tables and chairs set up in the middle of the room, where you can bring books to read and study. Along one side, there were single cubicles set up, if you wanted more privacy while you worked, and the other side of the room had many comfy armchairs and couches where you could lounge and read. I grabbed the first book I touched off a random shelf, and parked my butt on an armchair. I chose a chair that gave me a view of both entrances into this area, so I could see everyone who was coming and going. It was a genius plan.

There was a huge fancy, old-looking clock that overlooked the room. If time worked the same way here as it did back home, I sat there for about five hours. Five long hours of people-watching.

Lotus would kill me if I didn't describe what the clothing was like. The library patrons and tourists were dressed differently than in our modern style. Whether it was a different past or future, it was hard to tell. The best way I could describe everyone's outfit is this - watch an old Star Trek episode from the 1980s or 1990s. What the creators thought the future would look like back then, but still looks old and dated, is what I would describe this Earth's current fashion. Clothes just had weird lines, and some outfits looked like pyjamas. Cameras, maps, souvenirs, and comfortable shoes let you know who the tourists were. Their technology looked different than ours, but I wouldn't know if it was more advanced or inferior to what we have now.

During my five long hours of hopeful people-watching, I couldn't even tell you what book sat in my lap. I turned pages to make it look like I was a productive member in the reading/study area, but I don't remember ever looking down at it. I do remember that it felt old, so I was gentle and respectful with every page I turned.

I didn't get hungry, thirsty, or feel the need to find a bathroom, for the approximately seven to eight hours I had been there. I had to make a mental note to see if I felt any of these urges on my next trip. I have eaten and drank stuff before. I ate at the music festival with Cami, and more recently, there was the punch, but I can't remember if I ever felt like I needed to eat or drink.

I wasn't hungry or thirsty, but I was feeling disappointed and a little pissed at myself. This stupid, silly, pathetic obsession made me waste what could have been one of my best trips to date. Or maybe the worst, but I will never know. I had been there so long, but I had not taken advantage of the scenery, or truly appreciated where I was. I could have read about this world, learned about its history, and done some research that could perhaps help me better understand where I travel to or even find answers to how I travel. I should have gone outside, to see if there were acres of manicured lawns, or if I were in the middle of a busy city, with other fun tourist attractions. When I decided I had sat long enough and I should be doing all the above, it was too late. My body told me it was time to go, and the nausea brought me home.

Screw you Rude Boy.

The approximate eight hours I was away, equalled four days back home. When I was describing my trip to Lotus, I kept the search for Rude Boy to myself. I was so ashamed of how I acted. I would tell her eventually because being ashamed of how I felt is one thing, but keeping secrets from her after we both pledged to never do so, felt worse.

I told myself that this nonsense with Rude Boy had to be over. I made a pledge and promised myself that I was finally going to let go of this matter and that I would fully immerse myself in my next adventure.

It turns out, I am a big freakin' liar!

LIAR!

I travelled again in late April. I arrived at a huge shopping mall. Think Mall of America size, but this felt more grand and very elegant. I arrived on the third floor, next to a balcony. The balcony formed a circular shape, and when I looked up, I saw many similar balconies above me. In the middle of the balconies flowed an amazing waterfall. I knew I had to investigate how many levels this shopping centre had, and where the waterfall began.

I couldn't tell you the answer to this.

When I had my bearings and my head felt normal, (I feel dizzy for the first few moments of arrival every time I travel), I was about to start exploring when a nagging feeling wouldn't leave me alone. My stomach started to feel upset and I felt a panic wash over me. My mind betrayed me with the intrusive thought "What if he was here *this* time?"

No!

I said out loud "Screw you Rude Boy" to fight against whatever power was trying to take hold of me. (And then I apologized to the actual boy who was standing beside me, who thought my yelling was directed toward him.)

But my mind and body worked against me again. I could not escape that awful feeling that if I didn't look for him, I could miss him. This could very well be a place where a teenage boy could be found.

So that is what I did. I walked around for approximately five or so hours. I don't remember the shops, I can't recall any attractions, or even what people were wearing. (Sorry Lotus.) I concentrated on faces, and when I couldn't see faces, I chased down anyone who was tall with dark wavy hair, which resulted in a lot of awkward moments and many embarrassing situations. I continued my search until I left. I was a mean, teen, pathetically obsessed stalker machine.

When I returned home and was finally able to talk to Lotus, I had to come clean about this trip and the last. I desperately needed help getting over whatever this was I was going through. Lotus shared a few choice words and phrases with me, then spent a few minutes lecturing me about why I should never keep secrets from her, and then threatened me for another few minutes, explaining what would happen if I ever kept anything from her again. With all that housekeeping out of the way, we were finally able to talk about my situation and dig deeper into the issue. We both realized this would need an extensive review, that could not be done over the phone. I was able to convince my parents to have Lotus over for a few nights the upcoming weekend.

When Lotus finally arrived, after we gathered all the junk food we needed, and my parents stopped hovering, we finally got to work. We once again analyzed the school dance. Every movement I made, he made, my dance partner made, and his dance partner made. We took note of every emotion I felt and when I felt it and talked extensively about the "No!" I swear I heard him yell. We then proceeded to do the same thing for my last two trips. I retraced every thought and emotion I had that I could remember.

After two nights of going over all the evidence, Lotus came to the conclusion that I was suffering from a bad case of teenage crushing. I vehemently denied her crush diagnosis, but I did admit he was one of the hottest guys I have ever seen. Again, that doesn't mean I have a crush on him. I can appreciate looks without it meaning anything! Just like I can admit that Lotus is beautiful, but my love for her is purely platonic. My conclusion was inconclusive. I still felt that I wasn't any closer to having any definite answers that would guide me as to what to do about this situation. I still have a nagging feeling that there is something bigger at play.

We may have disagreed with what it all meant, but we both agreed that I needed to try to let it go, and she would help me do that. She reminded me that she was only a text away, so if I started to feel crazy and obsessed, I should text her immediately, and she could set me straight.

We also both agreed that I didn't have time for this nonsense right now because my seventeenth birthday was coming up very soon, and we needed to plan for that, which would include weeks of manipulating and begging my parents to either have Lotus back for another weekend, or better yet, for me to visit her again in the city.

The manipulating and planning only took a week and a half.

There may be some confusion as to why I now have to beg and manipulate to see friends. (I told you

I would be all over the place while writing this. There is too much to remember!) When we first moved and everything changed, they would allow Lotus and me to see each other whenever schedules allowed us. Lotus's social life did slow this down, but when my time away started to not coincide with the time here at home, my parents freaked out about it, and pretty much put me on lockdown. They never liked me leaving and hated every time I did, so they came to the conclusion that if I lived the most boring, lonely life ever, my travelling wouldn't be triggered as often. My parents think their plan has worked, though I doubt they would admit it if it didn't. For the record, I think their plan is full of crap.

My parents said no to all my birthday requests in the beginning, but they always do. I know now to wait a few days before casually bringing up again whatever it is I am asking for. You have to lay the groundwork, and then play all your cards. I really overplayed the "Birthday Card" this year. For some reason, turning seventeen felt like a big birthday to me, and I let them know this, constantly. I played the "Woe Is Me Card." I mentioned a few times how I am feeling a bit trapped and claustrophobic. The "Reminder Card" came out. They needed to remember that the last time I was in the city was almost six months ago. The "I Deserve This" card. All my school assignments were finally up to date and I wasn't behind on anything. I even read a few extra books that were not on my assigned reading list.

I should mention, all these cards were played after the "What The Hell" card, the "You Are Ruining My Life" card, "This Sucks, Do You Even Want Me To Be Happy?" card, and the famous "I Should Just Run Away" card, which is so cliché, and dramatic, but I was sixteen, and on forever house arrest, so it happened.

After a week and a half of my drama, my parents actually came to me to let me know I could stay with Lotus for two nights, the weekend before my birthday. I learned that my parents had scheduled some meetings during those days, so it actually worked out better if I came with them. They would not tell me what the meetings were for, or with whom, and it felt like I was being dropped off to be babysat, but I took the win regardless. I was going to ignore my parents' weird, sketchy behaviour, and enjoy my birthday celebrations.

SEVENTEEN

I had the best time with Lotus. It was just your typical girl hangout, well our typical can't leave the house, hangout. We watched our favourite shows and movies, baked a cake, made funny videos, and helped Lotus pick out a dress and makeup for another upcoming dance. She even scored us a few bottles of champagne, and we toasted each other's birthdays. Her birthday is in June, so we decided to make this a double birthday celebration, because we knew asking my parents to bring me here again so soon was not going to happen.

I'm not even sure if this is worth mentioning, but there were a few times when we were together when Lotus would have to stop herself from bursting into tears. It happened at the most sporadic times, like when we would be having a laughing fit, talking, or just being quiet on our phones. It happened a few times a day, so I became worried. When I asked her what was wrong she kept dismissing it, saying it was nothing, that she was just having an emotional day. We had promised countless times to never keep anything from each other, but I felt she was holding back on me. Her love life was fine. As far as I knew, Lotus and her girlfriend were still dating and hadn't fought recently. Her grades were good, no one was bothering her at school, and she had all the latest trendy clothes she wanted, so there was no reason, that I could think of, that would make her burst into such random sadness. I left it alone, but I think one day I will bring this up with her again, and maybe she will come clean when she is ready to talk about it. I'm a little upset that she wouldn't talk about it now though, but maybe her explanation was the truth. I mean, PMS is a bitch, and add that to our teenage hormones, and we are bound to have days where we just want to cry. It's possible it might be becoming a habit for me to build things up in my mind and make something out of nothing, but I have that gut feeling about this, like I do with Rude Boy. If there is an update about this, I will make sure to write about it.

A few days later, I turned seventeen. Even though it was just a quiet day spent with my parents, it felt extravagant, and I was spoiled. I can tell they really listened when I said I felt this was a big birthday for me. Mom baked me the most gorgeous delicious cake. It was a strawberries and cream cake, which I have been dying to try ever since I saw one on a baking competition show. She also made all my favourite finger foods, and Dad drove to get my favourite pizza from the town he works in. Dad also took the day off, and the three of us spent the day eating, playing my favourite board games, and binge-watching all the Pitch Perfect movies. It was pretty perfect.

And that brings me to the present. Finally! My hand has been seriously cramping from all this writing.

My birthday was a month ago. To my parents' delight, I have not travelled since April.

I guess moving forward, I will be treating this like

a diary. I'm not going to write in it every day, because my daily life isn't worth writing about. I started writing in this journal to document my travels, and now that I feel I have fully explained the past, moving forward, I can document my travels as they happen, or anything related to them.

WITCH HUNT

I t is mid-July. I just got back from another trip.

I have so much to unpack from this trip, my mind is spinning, and my hands won't stop shaking. Holy crap, buckle up!

I left on a Sunday morning. I was lying in bed watching my phone when I got the familiar physical symptoms telling me I was about to leave. I had enough time to find my parents, who were in the kitchen making coffee, said my goodbyes, and then I was gone.

Up until that morning, every departure has taken me to a place that was pleasant, safe, and always had the potential to be a positive experience. Every place was beautiful, with friendly people and pleasurable activities or attractions. I always felt a sense of joy, warmth and love in every location I have been to. If I didn't have a good time, it was by my own doing. (Remember my dark days, or being dumb and looking for a non-existent boy.)

When I arrived at my latest destination, before I could catch my bearings and let my head adjust, I could sense the chaos before my other senses woke up. First I heard screaming, crying, yelling, loud footfalls, and crackling noises. I smelled wood burning and heavy earthy farm-like smells. I felt cold wind and blasts of heat. My eyes soon adjusted to complete the scene and it was horrifying. I was transported back to what I would imagine villages looked like in the late 1600s. With the brief look I got of the village, it looked to me like it was a small, poor farming settlement. The buildings were somewhat close together and looked like they were made of wood, clay and grass. Honestly, just google what a typical village in the 1690s looked like, and I guarantee that is what it looked like. I'm not an expert on this time period, I had to do some internet searches myself to find a time in our history that was comparable to where I was.

At first, I could have sworn that I was transported back to the actual Salem witch trials that happened from 1662-1663 here on our Earth. (Thank you internet for the info!) During that time, in Salem Massachusetts, in the US, there were actual trials to prove whether one was a witch or not. But unlike our Earth, the dreadful scene playing before me contained no such trials. It looked as if the self-righteous were playing judge, jury, and executioner on the spot.

I watched with shock and horror as men and women were dragged from their homes. Children were screaming as they were being ripped out of their parent's arms, and either given to other possible family members or put in a horse-drawn cart if they were about to be orphaned. I think I arrived early to mid-morning, as it looked like some people were being dragged out of their houses still wearing their sleep clothing. As the men and women were being escorted away from their homes and families, other villagers were chanting "witch witch…" and pointing at the accused. Some homes were being set on fire. Why some homes were chosen and others weren't, it wasn't clear to me, but now that I am sitting here in reflection, I could only assume that someone felt the entire home or plot of land needed to be cleansed.

The accused were being herded over to a massive tree that stood alone in a clearing, just past the little village. This tree had many branches, all thick and strong. Some men were climbing the tree, with ropes in hand. They were preparing the tree to hang everyone they accused of being a witch.

I couldn't stay to watch, I needed to get out of there. My mind was telling my body to run, but I was stuck, frozen in place with disbelief, panic and fear. Fight or flight my ass. One of those would have been useful.

Tears started to sting my eyes, and then fall, as I was forced to continue to watch the horrifying spectacle as my body betrayed me.

If only I could understand my gift. How I travel, or why I travel. I want to say I have been searching for answers all these years, but really, I don't even know where or how to start looking for answers. Is it even a gift? It can't be to bring me to such an event. Would I subconsciously put myself in danger? Am I even in control of any of this?

I somehow managed to close my eyes and tried to will myself to leave. Pleading with whatever part of me (or something else) that was responsible for bringing me home. I whispered, "Please let me leave" on repeat, hoping no one noticed the terrified, frozen girl standing amongst the chaos.

A hand grabbed onto my upper arm and my eyes flew open as I watched a tall, broad-shouldered man start to drag me away. My body finally decided to react, and I tried to pull away, but he was strong, and my effort to fight went almost unnoticed, except his grip became tighter, and he started to walk faster.

I was being ushered towards an old wooden shed. This is it, I thought to myself. This is where he was going to have his way with me, and then kill me, or hand me off to the executioners at the tree.

Before I could further protest at this realization, the shed door was being opened and I was thrown in. I quickly spun around to confront my captor. He had his back turned to me, while he was locking us inside the shed. I used this opportunity to look for anything I could use as a weapon. Thankfully this shed kept many tools, and I quickly chose a hammer to arm myself. I stood there ready, waiting for him to turn around as he fumbled to barricade the door further.

It was then that I found my voice.

"If you even try to fucking touch me, I'm going to hammer your fucking brains in!"

I shouted in the most intimidating voice and language I could muster. It seemed to work because my would-be assailant stopped fussing with the door, froze and put his hands in the air.

As I was about to bark my next command, he spoke.

"What are you doing?" He asked in a steady voice with a hint of annoyance.

"What does it look like I'm doing?" I answered with bewilderment. "Isn't it obvious? I'm trying to escape from you and your torture shed!"

"Escape?" he asked. He was facing away, but I could tell he was frustrated with me. He took one hand, pinched the bridge of his nose, and ran his fingers through his hair, before putting it back in the air.

"Oh, I'm sorry, are you frustrated with me? You

grab me, shove me in a shed, lock me inside with you, and you are frustrated? My apologies. Next time, I'll remember my place, and just give in to your every toxic masculine demand." I was on a roll. Dad always taught me to be loud and combative if I ever found myself in a situation with someone who was trying to take advantage of me. I feel like he would have been proud.

"I'm not trying to hurt you, I'm trying to help you!" he said, as he started to turn around.

"Don't you dare turn around!" I yelled, and to my surprise, he stopped. "How does any of this look like you are helping me?"

"You gave me no choice. I was trying to get your attention when you were standing outside. I was practically yelling into your ear, but you were in some sort of trance or something. So I grabbed your arm and brought you here before anyone could see you." he explained, his patience seemingly growing thin.

"What do you mean, before anyone could see me?" Was I missing something?

"For F–, will you just look at yourself!" He blurted out, patience gone, frustration winning over.

With no mirrors at my disposal, I looked down at my outfit. I saw nothing crazy or out of the ordinary. I was wearing my black yoga pants, a grey tank top, my black oversized zip-up hoodie, and my grey slippers that look like Ugg boots.

I'm ashamed to say, it took me a few minutes to put this together.

"Holy Shit!" I finally reacted. I didn't change!? My clothing always changed when I travelled, and I must have taken that fact for granted, to not have noticed I was still in my modern-age loungewear.

When I was finally making this realization aloud, my captor, or rescuer began to slowly turn around.

By this point, my body was developing into a full-blown panic attack. I felt like I couldn't breathe, and the room was starting to spin. I was losing control.

"Do you think that maybe you can put the hammer down now? I promise, I only want to help."

If you have ever had a panic attack before, you know that you can't focus on anything but trying to breathe. You become completely irrational, and while it is a mental attack, your physical symptoms are all too real. So when I was asked to do the simple task of putting the hammer down, while trying to figure out why my clothes didn't change, while my mind was trying to process what I saw outside, all while trying to force my body to breathe and remain conscious, it all became too much, and my mind broke. I must have looked like a crazy person. I was told later that I looked frozen (again), except for the forced breaths, while I just stared at the hammer in my hand.

I was aware that my (now) protector was slowly walking toward me. When he reached me, he slowly reached for my hand that held the hammer. Instead of taking it from me, he placed his hand on mine and ever so gently, slowly guided my hand so the hammer lay at my side, instead of remaining threateningly in the air like it was.

Now that I am reliving this moment, this move was presumably calculated to gain my trust. He probably realized that if he took the hammer out of my hand, it could startle me and I may become more defensive, but by helping me lower the hammer and allowing me to keep hold of it, I would keep that sense of security I felt while threatening him with it. Am I making sense? Disarming me = threatened. Keeping me armed = trust.

Smart move.

Guiding my hand down had another consequence whether intended by him or not. His touch helped ground me, and I was able to slightly calm the panic, which allowed me to take my first easy breath in minutes. With that breath, I was finally able to look up.

Impossibly dark eyes met mine.

DANGER

Rude Boy!

"Holy Shit, it's you!" I blurted out. I have been looking for this dude, for what, almost a year, and this is what I managed to say to him. Way to keep it cool! "I have so many questions!"

"We don't have time for this right now" he responded, speaking quickly and quietly. "Why would you show up here dressed like that? We need to get you changed now!"

"This isn't my fault! I don't have control over any of this." I bit back, matching his quiet tone.

We both started to look around frantically, to find anything I could drape over me, but this shed only contained farming equipment.

"Ok, I saw some clothes on a clothesline a few houses down. I'm going to run out and grab whatever I can, and hurry back. I need you to hide."

"You can't leave me! What if they find me? I'll be dragged to that hanging tree immediately!" I protested.

"We don't have a choice. We can't stay here. There are a few groups of men who are re-checking every building, a second and third time, looking for anyone hiding from execution. I'm going to leave the door open when I'm gone." he started to explain.

I opened my mouth to protest but he was quick to interrupt.

"If they see the door open, they will assume this shed has already been checked, and it might buy us some time. I can tell that you are freaking out, but you have to trust me. I'll be right back. I won't leave you, I promise."

I did trust him. I can't explain why, but my instincts were telling me I could. I was too terrified to speak, but I managed to nod my head, yes, to show I understood. He helped me hide behind a barrel, and then he was gone.

Every part of my body was shaking as I crouched down on the floor. The screaming and crying outside had not let up but grew louder and more desperate. I closed my eyes and did my best to plug my ears, and started to will myself to leave again. Whether Rude Boy was coming back or not, if I could leave, I was going to. If I could find him twice while travelling, I was confident I would bump into him again, and I would apologize then for leaving. He would have to understand. He wasn't in danger here, but I was. I would make him understand.

Heavy, large hands fell on my knees, gently and then vigorously shaking me. I finally looked up to find Rude Boy trying to snap me out of another trance-like state. He had returned, with an arm full of fabric.

"We have run out of time," he said while grabbing my elbows, and pulling me to my feet. "We need to get you dressed now! There is a search party heading this way, and they are being thorough with their searches. I barely made it here without being seen"

He started unzipping my sweater in an attempt to rush me. "Ok, Ok, I get it, we have to hurry, but I can dress myself," I assured him. "Could you at least turn around? I'm not in the habit of undressing around boys."

"We seriously have no time for modesty right now," he said as he turned me around so my back faced him. "Take off your clothes and I will hand you these. I will do my best not to look."

I could hear a group of loud, angry men getting closer, so I didn't argue. I started whipping off my clothes in record time.

"Your bra too," he whispered timidly.

As if he knew what I was going to say, he continued, "I'm hoping that we will escape here without being seen, but if there is a chance we are found, and your bra strap is showing, I don't know how we are going to explain Victoria's Secret to these irrational town folk."

He had a point. I made quick work with ALL my upper clothing and was immediately handed a long off-white robe. I slipped it on over my head. It had long sleeves and a collar that could button to the neck. It fell to the ground, so I took advantage of the length to take off my yoga pants, without showing anything. I decided my underwear was not up for discussion and would protest it heavily if Rude Boy mentioned it, but he did not. Because we were out of time, while I was fighting my way out of my yoga pants, Rude Boy came behind me and tied a long brown apron onto my front. It wasn't a complete outfit, but it would pass.

"I couldn't find you any socks, or shoes, so you will have to go barefoot for now. I promise I will come up with something later, but we must leave now."

He gathered all my modern clothing and wrapped them in a dirty old cloth he brought in with clothes he found.

We heard the group of men approaching the door to the shed. We were trapped and out of time. Rude Boy was quick to action and started to kick at a loose board at the back of the shed. After his third kick, the board gave way and a small opening was made. It was just large enough for us to crawl through.

When I crawled my way out of the shed, Rude Boy immediately lifted me up and pushed me against the wall, so he could assess the situation. He had a better idea of the town's layout than I did, so I decided to keep my mouth shut and do what he said. My instincts told me that I was not getting out of here alive without his help.

He waited until the men entered the shed before we ran off. He grabbed my hand, and we started running in the direction that the men just came from. Smart, or so I thought until I realized we were running towards the houses that were on fire. I started choking, and breathing became harder.

As if he knew I was struggling, he said, "Just don't let go of my hand!" as he continued to guide me.

We ran as fast as we could without drawing too much attention to ourselves. Some women and children ran past us, trying to escape the smoke and heat. I was worried we looked suspicious as we ran towards the fire, while everyone else was running away from it, but no one noticed us, or didn't care to notice. Most people were in survival mode. Rude Boy used this opportunity to throw my clothes he was still carrying into one of the house fires.

We had made our way past three burning houses. When we found a break in the smoke, I became aware of what Rude Boy's plan might be. We were making our way to the edge of the village where the forest began. The furthermost house was on fire. If we could get behind that house undetected, we could use the smoke to shield us as we ran across the small clearing and into the forest's cover.

Unfortunately, there were no houses on fire from where we currently stood, to where we needed to be. That sounded terrible. It was unfortunate for us that we ran out of cover, but fortunate for whoever lived in those houses.

I was led to the side of the house where we crouched down to plan our next move, and to catch our breath. When we thought it might be clear to move, we heard one of the groups of angry loud men getting closer.

"I told you they were being thorough" he whispered, as his head darted side to side, looking for our way out.

The voices were getting closer. We had to move.

Rude Boy had us back on our feet, slowly backing up to the back corner of the house. We both had a hard time determining which direction the angry mob was coming from. Suddenly, I felt a push, and I fell to the ground behind the building.

"What are you hiding boy?" said an unfamiliar, gruff voice.

"What do you mean?" my so-called protector answered back, while I wiped dirt off my hands and knees. I wanted to yell at him and ask if that push was necessary but his stiff demeanour told me I needed to be quiet. The house I was pushed behind backed into a tall wooden fence. I had nowhere to run to. My life, once again, was in his hands.

"Don't play dumb with us boy, we saw you hide somethin' behind you" answered the spokesperson for the mob. "If it's a witch yer hidin', we'll hang ya both!"

"Ok, ok, look, I promise I'm not hiding a witch, but..." Before he finished what he was going to say, he grabbed my arm and pulled me out of hiding, to face the angry group of men.

There were only seven in this group. I thought the group was larger, but it's possible they split up to quickly cover more ground. Regardless, we were outnumbered.

When the group of men saw me, they made all sorts of noises, from gasps, cheers, and grunts, and said some very perverted things I wish never to hear ever again.

Rude Boy finished "I saw her standing all alone, and I thought, no one would miss her for a little while." While talking, he placed me in front of him, slipped his arm around my waist, and pulled me against him, which was met with more approving noises from the mob. He grabbed my face with his other hand, pinching my chin. "She is just so pretty, I just thought, maybe I could, you know, get to know her better..."

I knew he was putting on an act to put off our potential attackers, but his act was a little too convincing for me. I didn't need to "play along." I was so disgusted by his words and felt pure revulsion from the mob's reaction. I struggled against his hold and got a few good jabs in before he readjusted his grip, and I could no longer move. How was he this strong? I really was at his mercy.

"This way is clear" the group's leader yelled to the rest of the mobs, who were scattered about. Before he continued on with his search, he gave Rude Boy a wink, and the other men showed their approval with some rude gestures and creepy smiles.

Rude Boy didn't let go of me until the groups of

men moved further down the houses. Before he could say anything, I spun around and slapped him across the face, as hard as I could. Without missing a beat, he grabbed my hand and started leading me toward the forest.

"You can resist me all you want, and hate me all you want, but I am not letting go until we reach the woods. Your struggle just adds to our new cover, so do what you need to do."

He spoke so evenly, and without emotion. It hurt, but I didn't know why. It's not like I actually know this person. It felt like maybe he feels like he has to save me, and is pissed off by this obligation.

We walked at a fast pace to the forest. Running might draw too much attention after our encounter. If we ran, the group of men may figure out they were deceived. By walking, it looks like he was bringing me to the woods, to do exactly what he implied he would do.

We were almost at the forest's edge when I heard women screaming. It was coming from close to where we were just hiding, so it was loud. Loud, desperate, heartbreaking, terrified screaming. The self-righteous perverted assholes were able to find more so-called "witches" who were in hiding.

I tugged back on Rude Boy's hand. "We have to try to help them!" I yelled desperately.

"No, we don't," he answered back, without missing a step.

"We can't just leave them! They are going to kill them!" By this time I was sobbing uncontrollably.

He didn't respond and continued leading us to the forest, in silence.

STARTING OVER

We hit the tree line, but he didn't stop walking. We walked in silence for another ten minutes before he finally stopped and let go of me.

He was the first to speak. "We can't stay here, we have to keep moving to a safer distance, but I thought you might want to rest your feet."

My feet. I forgot I was barefoot. If my feet were in pain, I wasn't able to feel them yet. I wasn't able to feel much of anything at the moment. I assured him my feet would be fine, so we kept walking.

We walked in silence for a very long time. I kept sneaking glances at him, while he kept his gaze straight ahead and focused. If he looked at me at all during this time, I didn't catch him doing it. If I had to guess, at least three hours had gone by before we felt safe enough to stop and have a proper rest. We stopped by a stream, still deep in the woods, so there was plenty of tree coverage to protect us if we were being pursued. I assumed we weren't, or else we would have heard the hunting party by now. He must have had the same assumption, at least I think he may have. I still couldn't bring myself to speak to him.

I sat at the stream's edge, so I could wash my feet and hands.

"I'm sorry." Again, he was the first to break the silence. He had sat down beside me.

"For which part?" I managed to say, surprised, yet proud of my boldness.

"Those men would not have let us go unless I stooped to their level. You have to believe me. If they thought I was hiding you for any other purpose, they would assume you were a witch and both of us would have been dragged to that tree to be hung."

"Did you have to get so handsy!" I muttered, rather ungratefully.

"First, I want to apologize for what I said about you, and for what you had to witness the men say and do. Although it was necessary, I hope you know that if there was another way out of that situation, anything else I could have done, I would have done it."

He continued, "Second, I want to apologize for grabbing you. Again, I tried to hold you in a way to satisfy the men, without being too inappropriate with you. If there was anything else I could have done…"

"You would have done it, I know, I get it." I finished for him.

I probably sounded like a complete bitch. The truth was that my brain was still processing EVERYTHING that just happened. It was a lot, in such a short amount of time. I needed to feel all the emotions and let my mind sort out exactly how I felt about each thing that happened.

I prepared myself for the "I was right about everything, and I saved you, so now maybe stop being so ungrateful and get over it" speech from him. To his credit, he didn't say anything more. He just stayed sitting beside me quietly.

After about a half hour of silence, I started to cry. Awesome. Out of all the emotions, this is what my brain landed on. I guess it decided that in order to process everything, this emotional release was needed.

To my surprise, he let me cry. I mean, he didn't do the typical guy thing, where they tell you, "You're ok, shh shh," because obviously, I was not ok. He just sat there and let me cry, without interference, as if he knew that was exactly what I needed.

Who is this guy?

After my therapeutic cry session, and the remaining tears and snot were wiped from my face, (I am not a pretty crier) I finally found some clarity and was able to sort out my thoughts, and found my voice again.

With great humility, I turned to him. "I'm so sorry if, at any point, I came across as unappreciative to you. I am beyond grateful for what you did for me today. You not only saved my life, but you saved it more than once."

I then went on to explain that I was having a hard time coping with everything and asked if he was willing to talk things through, and if he was, I promised to leave my attitude behind.

He laughed at the last part. "Your attitude was excusable, but I would love to start over".

"I have a bajillion questions, but there is something I need to ask first, to clear the air." I needed to know what kind of person he was, besides the whole rescue of a damsel in distress kind of guy.

"You want to know why we didn't try to help anyone." he quickly chimed in.

"Yes." I was starting to think he could read my thoughts. 'Must not think about how hot he is' I quickly thought to myself, because that is where my brain went, even after everything that *just* happened. I'm so disappointed in myself.

"The easy answer is that we were outnumbered. If we tried to help anyone, we would not be here right now talking to each other. It was just too dangerous." he started to explain.

"What is the not easy answer" I interrupted.

"It is more like the complicated answer." He began. "It has been my experience when navigating through the many places we get to visit, to never interfere."

'So he is like me,' I quickly thought to myself.

"Is there a set of rules I should be aware of? A guidebook I forgot to pick up, or got lost in the mail? And what do you mean by 'interfere'? When we were talking to those men, would that not be considered interfering? And why did it feel so easy for you to ignore the cries for help?"

"There is taking an active part, and then there is interfering. Interfering would be changing how an event is to take place, possibly changing the course of history. Say we could help a few, or even all the people here today. It would be a win for today, but what if our actions had more severe consequences in the near or distant future? Does that make sense?" He asked.

I nodded, and in return, I asked, "Do you know this for sure, or is this a theory?

"I guess it's my theory.'" he answered. "I could be wrong, but from most of my travels, I have always had the impression that we are merely observers."

"We are observers who should not interfere, but

taking part is ok?" I waited for him to finish clarifying his theory.

"Taking part seems harmless to me. It doesn't seem to have any life-shattering or timeline-interrupting consequences. Especially if locals started the interaction with us first. So trying to stop an unnecessary, violent, heartbreaking event like where we find ourselves today would be interfering. And I promise, I was moved more than I let on by their cries. My survival mode took over, and when that happens, I sometimes become cold and calculating." He paused for a moment, in what felt like self-reflection. When he spoke again, his demeanour changed slightly, and he spoke with a smile. "On the other hand, accepting an invitation to dance with someone, at a school function, or playing innocent games at a garden party, is what I consider, just taking part."

"You are the boy from the party at the castle!" I wasn't aware that I said this out loud, but he was quick to confirm with a head nod.

"Were you on a trip, when we first met or is that your home?" I thought this was a good place to start my questioning.

"It was a trip, and I remember you, like you remember me. I think I somehow knew you were like me, so I was drawn to you. You looked at everything like it was brand new, and didn't take any of the splendour for granted, like the other kids did. I wanted to speak to you, to confirm my suspicions, but you were gone before I had the courage to do so." He explained.

"I honestly didn't think anyone else could do what I do," I said. "It wasn't until the school dance, when I saw you, that I thought it could be a possibility. But even then, I wasn't sure if you were....well, you, the boy from the garden."

He explained to me how he saw me and recognized me first. My looks have matured a lot, but I still very much look like that little girl he once played with. It was my "child-like wonder" he said that confirmed that I had to be the same girl. Apparently, I still have no chill and can't wipe the awestruck look off my face when I go to a new place. The staring at me while we danced was intentional so that I could maybe recognize him too. When I had my panic episode, he didn't realize it was because I *did* recognize him, so he left the gym to walk off his disappointment of me not knowing who he was. He also thought he creeped me out and lost any chance to talk to me. I can confirm that when I left, he did in fact yell 'NO!' which was such a relief to hear because I fantasized about that moment every day. No, I did not tell him that.

I did admit that I had named him "Rude Boy" after that encounter and apologized profusely for it. He laughed it off and was understanding as to why that was his temporary name.

I was about to ask what his actual name was, when, as if he could read my mind, interrupted our conversation to bring us back into our present predicament. Before we continued talking, he wanted to quickly check our surroundings, to make sure we were as safe as we currently felt, and to move us to a spot along the stream that might provide a bit more shelter. He thought it best, and I agreed, to stay here for the rest of the day/night, and start looking for another town at first daylight. The witch hunt hysteria could have infected other neighbouring villages, so it was best to wait for a new day.

When we finally got settled, we continued talking. We talked through a bit more of what we just witnessed in the town a few hours ago, until I decided I couldn't talk or think about it anymore. I brought the conversation back to the dance and what happened after. Even though I felt like I had more questions for him than he had for me, he managed to steer the conversation, so that I was doing a lot of the talking. I admitted that I searched for him at the next few places I went to, and then had convinced myself that I read too much into the events of the dance. To my surprise, and utter glee, he admitted that he looked for me as well.

When I was looking for him, I waited until I travelled and searched for him at whatever destination I arrived at. He explained when he was looking for me, he was actively jumping from one destination to the next, trying to encounter me.

He can control it! Holy shit!

Not only is he in control of when he leaves to go on our unique trips, but he can leave that place whenever he wants. He also explained that he could revisit places he has already been to. The only thing he does not control is the clothing. Together, we still can't figure out how that works. When I asked how he controls his ability, his answers were a bit vague. He mentioned how it comes down to a feeling. He thinks of going, closes his eyes, feels some sort of energy, and then is somewhere else when he opens his eyes. When I tried to clarify what he meant by feeling, he brought the conversation back to me.

From his viewpoint, he was fascinated by the fact that I had no control over any of it. He assumed I had control over the clothing and thought I was being careless when I showed up to a witch hunt in my normal clothes.

"So you could leave right now if you wanted to?" I asked in disbelief.

"Yes, this second," he replied.

"Why didn't you leave right away, when you saw what was happening when you first got here?" I asked.

"I wanted to, and I was going to, but I decided to do a quick search of the village, just in case I happen to see you. After about a half hour, I decided it was becoming too dangerous to stay, and I assumed that if you did arrive here, you would probably choose to leave right away too. That was when I saw you, and the rest, well....you know."

We then spent the next few hours talking about where we have been and what we have experienced. I was fascinated by his travels, and he was entertained by mine. Surprisingly, we had not been to any of the same destinations, besides the dance and castle, which tells me there are countless more places I have yet to explore, Infinite even.

It became dark, sooner than I thought it would. We decided trying to build a fire would be a bad idea. We didn't want to attract any unwanted attention, but luckily the moon was full, and the sky was cloudless, so we had plenty of light.

I had tried many times to ask where he calls home, if he knew anyone else who could travel like us, or simply, his name, but these questions were expertly dodged by him asking follow-up questions about something we already talked about. Or he would interrupt me, thinking he heard something, and then continue to talk after a few minutes when he felt it was safe, acting like I never asked anything. He may think he got away with it, but I just let it go, for now. He must have had a reason for avoiding my inquiries. We really didn't know each other after all, so spilling our entire life story wouldn't be smart. So I stopped asking, and kept the conversation light and on the topic of travelling.

The annoying thing was at this point, he knew my name and I had given it to him freely, and without thought.

It had to have been well after midnight when I realized I should feel cold and tired, but I didn't. I also had not been hungry or had any other natural urges. I asked if he felt the same, or didn't feel, and he confirmed it worked the same way for him.

Before I was ready, the sun began to rise, which meant that he would want to start walking again. I don't know if time worked differently where we were, but the night went by very fast. Or maybe it was just so easy to talk with him that time only felt like it sped up. I was so comfortable in our little spot by the stream and could have easily stayed there for many more hours conversing with him. I was hoping he felt the same, but I never got the chance to ask if the feeling was mutual.

The familiar feeling of nausea crept up on me. How many times would my body betray me on this trip?

"Oh no! I think I'm leaving" I suddenly cried out, interrupting one of his stories.

"How much time do you have?" He asked, with an air of desperation.

"I don't know, it's different every time. Minutes, maybe seconds. Will I ever see you again?" I asked, hoping time could just stand still for a few minutes.

"Yes, I promise, we will see each other again soon," he reassured me, as he placed my hands in his.

"How?"

"Don't worry about the how, just know I'll find you!"

"Your name?" This was all I could spit out, the

94

nausea was getting stronger. I was out of time.

"My friends call me Gabe," I heard him say as he and my surroundings blurred out of existence.

GABE

I'm told when I was coming to, phasing back to my home reality, the first thing I said was "Gabe".

After Mom finished smothering me, and Dad was finished with his usual checkups, they insisted that I rest before I talk with anyone. For the first time, I agreed with them. I'm usually a little woozy, and a bit tired when I come back, but I can usually shake it off and find myself back to normal quite quickly. After this trip, I was exhausted. It had left an emotional and physical toll on me, and I was more than happy to sleep it off.

I was away for what I think was almost twenty-four hours, give or take a few hours. I'm told I was gone for six days here at home. I then slept for the next twenty hours.

When my parents felt I was finally well rested, they sat me down in the living room and asked (Mom reluctantly) about my trip. I burst into tears when I started my story. I think the trauma of witnessing that village's destruction, seeing and hearing all the victims, will stay with me for a long time. The story got easier to tell when Gabe made his entrance. I left out the men finding us part, but told them everything else.

"So Gabe is like you?" Mom wanted more

clarification.

"Yes, but no. He is a traveller like me, but is better at it. Or has more advanced abilities. I'm still not really sure." I was annoyed with my answer. I felt that I spent enough time with Gabe that I should have been able to answer this question with more detail. The truth was, besides a few key differences between us, I barely knew anything about him.

My parents were not very pleased about the Gabe part of my story, but they admit they are glad he was there to keep me safe. This pissed me off. Out of everything that happened, they focused on him. I saw horrible things that would put people in therapy for years, but let's focus on the boy I talked to. It makes sense, I guess. I have never been allowed to have a boyfriend or even go on a date, so I shouldn't be surprised by any of this.

They had reached the point where they were finished humouring me and left the room. Again, this is normal. Mom can only hear so much until she gets overwhelmed. On my way back to my room, I overheard my parents talking in the kitchen.

"We can't let her do this anymore. Now she is seeing a boy? We can't allow this to keep happening! There has to be SOMETHING we can do!" Mom sounded a bit frantic.

"You know there is nothing we can do. How many more doctors or specialists do you need to talk to, to finally come to terms with this?" Dad was the voice of reason. He kept his cool when Mom couldn't.

"When I 'finally come to terms with this' is the day that I have given up on my daughter, and that day is never going to come!" Mom stormed out of the kitchen. She was so upset, but she was always upset after I came back. I knew space was all she needed, so I decided to leave it alone.

My next plan of action, as always, was to call Lotus and give her all the juicy details of my latest adventure. She was so excited, and what I thought, a bit emotional when she answered the video call. I recapped everything, including the scary men part. I needed her to know everything I went through, so she could give me her honest assessment of Gabe.

We analyzed every single detail that I could remember, and together, we came up with the following results. His amazing good looks are not featured in the analysis, but I am making note of them now. (Holy crap he is so hot.)

The Gabe Assessment

He has more experience and knowledge about our way of travelling, so it would be beneficial, for educational purposes, to see him again.

He is brave and acts with integrity. He could have left me at any time, but chose to stay and help me.

I should still be cautious around him. I feel like I could put my trust in him, but Lotus warns that he could have gained my trust to potentially hurt me later. I will keep this in mind.

We both find it strange that he avoided answering a lot of my questions, or if he did answer, he was very vague with his details. (Ok, so maybe Lotus might be onto something about being careful.)

It is not lost on me that when I asked for his name when I was leaving him, he replied, "My friends call me Gabe." I didn't ask what his friends call him. Is this a nickname? Is it short for something else? Did he just declare us friends? Am I overthinking this, like I always do?

What is his name?
Who is he?

CONSPIRACY

It has been four and a half months since my last trip. Four and a half months since I became acquainted with Gabe.

My parents are happy. I mean, Mom hasn't cried in a very long time and is giving me more space than I usually get, so in that respect, it's a good thing. Dad has been coming home from work in a better mood. Together, my parents have been stealing kisses and acting all weird and loving. I haven't seen that in a while.

I should be overjoyed that our house feels a bit more like it used to. In the last couple of months there has been no heavy tension, whispered conversations, or loud arguments. But I can't help but feel that their newfound happiness is the direct result of my misery. I get they are happy that I have not gone anywhere, but do they have to flaunt it in front of me? Especially knowing that I want to see Gabe again.

I need to mention my new vitamin routine. When I got back from my last trip, after my Dad did his usual examination, a few days later he handed me a bottle of vitamins and said I needed to start taking them. He concluded that my body was starting to show physical signs of weakness from my travels, becoming depleted of many vitamins and nutrients, so I needed to take them daily. It made sense, I was so tired after the last time.

So why am I mentioning something so ordinary as taking daily vitamins, asked no one, because I'm literally writing this to myself...I believe my parents are conspiring against me.

At first, I didn't think it was a big deal that I had to take them. I didn't even think anything was off when my parents insisted I take it in front of them every day with my breakfast. I forgot to take it three days in a row, so obviously, I needed the reminder. It was when I started asking innocent questions that I became aware that something wasn't right.

When I forgot to take them, I asked Dad if he could get them in a gummy form. I don't think I would forget to take a daily vitamin if they were chewy and delicious. He told me my vitamins were a special blend, so they couldn't get them in any chewable form.

My "special blend" of vitamins also looks different than what a normal multivitamin looks like, at least any I have taken. Vitamins are usually a large solid pill of whatever colour, or come in a gummy form. Mine are capsules.

I also noticed that Mom put the pills in a small clear jar with a wooden stopper. When I asked why the extra work, and why not just keep them in their original bottle, Dad reminded me of Mom's love of unnecessary containers, to keep a certain aesthetic. While this is true, Mom loves taking things out of their original containers and putting them in expensive clear ones, I have never seen her do this with medication. I'm reminded of one of Dad's many lectures about how to properly store medication, making sure everything is labelled properly, so you know exactly what you are taking, proper doses, and to help keep track of expiration dates and blah blah blah. It is obvious they don't want me to see the original bottle.

Am I even taking vitamins? The growing evidence shows me I am not. The most damaging evidence is that I have not travelled. This is the longest I have gone without leaving for many years.

What am I taking?

Are they secretly drugging away my ability?

What about what I want?

I decided I was going to suppress my emotions, the best that I could, and approach this situation, the conspiracy against me, from an unemotional, scientific perspective. If I am to accuse my parents of any trickery, I need solid proof.

The Experiment

Title
Conspiracy - Fact or Fiction

Background
I was given vitamins to improve my health. My health has greatly improved, I have never felt better, but there have been side effects. I have not travelled in the last four and a half months. I believe my parents are lying to me, telling me I am taking a vitamin when they are giving me a drug with the intent to suppress, or completely block my ability to travel.

Aim
I am going to test whether I am being given a vitamin or an ability deterrent.

Hypothesis
I am predicting that I will uncover the truth, and prove my parents are providing me with medication other than vitamins.

Risk Assessment
My health
- My overall health may decline

Parents
- When I bring them my findings, will this put a strain on our relationship?
- Can I Forgive them?
- Will they trust me after my betrayal?

Method

Every morning when my parents watch me take my pill, I will do my best to hide it in my cheek. I will then take a small bite of food, to not cause suspicion, and when I wipe my face with a napkin, I will secretly spit out the pill into the napkin, crumble it up, and put it in the garbage when breakfast has concluded.

I estimate it will take a few weeks to a month for the drug to leave my body. I also understand that I may not be one hundred percent successful with hiding the pill, so I am aiming for an eighty percent success rate on pill avoidance. This means it may take longer for my abilities to return.

Results

After two months, my health declined slightly. I felt my energy levels drop, became tired more easily, had more mood swings, and had slightly more headaches.

I also was able to travel again.

Discussion

I was able to fake taking the pill with an eighty-five percent success rate.

I don't believe my parents had any suspicions as to what I was doing. Some mornings they don't even watch me take it. They have taken for granted my compliance, or indifference to taking the pill in the last six months, so it was too easy to deceive them. I almost felt bad about it at one point, until I reminded myself that they were the first to betray.

I also kept my physical symptoms hidden from my parents the best that I could, to not draw suspicion, and to keep their minds off my pill routine.

Conclusion

I was right!

I freakin' knew it!

I'm not crazy, this conspiracy, this act of complete betrayal, is fact.

BEACH DAY

I finally left in early February. It has been a very long six and a half months. The night before I left, I was taking part in my biannual Twilight marathon. I stayed up way too late, so the next morning I couldn't escape that tired feeling even after I was fully awake. (I have a thought, maybe a growing theory about this, that I will come back to later.) After breakfast, and my pill-taking fake out, I finally got the familiar feeling of nausea. I was able to let my parents know what was happening, then I was gone.

It has been a gloomy, harsh winter, so I was relieved to have landed in a place with warm weather and bright sunshine. I was on a busy beach. Actually, I was standing on a walkway at the beach. Immediately I looked down to see what I was wearing and was relieved to see my clothes had changed. I was wearing a pair of jean shorts and a black tank top. For once, it was an outfit I would actually pick out for myself, so I felt instantly at ease.

The beach was a beautiful, white sandy beach that looked meticulous and untouched, despite the number of beachgoers who had settled on it. Luxurious wooden cabanas, shaded with soft white linen, and furnished with comfortable lounge chairs, lined the beach. If you weren't lucky enough to get a cabana, huge beach umbrellas were scattered throughout the beach to offer a break from the sun. The umbrellas were either turquoise or a soft yellow in colour. I thought maybe I was at a fancy resort, as these structures were provided for everyone to use, but upon further investigation, I concluded that this was a public beach open to everyone. The many shops behind me, vendors along the walkways and a few parking lots in the distance brought me to that conclusion.

The sand was stunning on its own, but it selflessly partnered with a clear, light blue ocean that told me I was in a tropical climate. I had been to a few tropical destinations when I was a kid when our family actually took vacations, but this was an entirely different level of paradise.

You would think that a paved sidewalk and shops would cheapen the feel of this area, but it didn't. All the shop buildings were small huts, uniform in size, but not in colour. The different colours were bright, yet soft. Palm trees lined both sides of the walkway, and made themselves home between shops, and behind. There were no huge ugly buildings, hotels, or condos as far as I could see.

The shops had a steady flow of people entering and leaving, while the walking path had constant foot traffic, coming from both directions. Many street artists and small vendors were scattered along the path, as you would typically see at a beach destination. It was busy, and I was aware of the number of people that were around me, but it didn't feel overwhelming. I felt very calm, very at peace, and very relaxed. A stark comparison from my last journey of destruction and hate.

That feeling of relaxation didn't last. After I became familiar with my surroundings, or, after I probably stood there like an idiot with my mouth open, staring at everything and everyone for who knows how long, my thoughts turned to Gabe.

It has been almost seven months since I last saw him. Did time work the same way for him? Has it been that long, if not longer wherever he lives? What if he thought I had ghosted him?! I really thought we had a connection, but maybe I misread everything. Except, he promised he would see me again. I'm still not sure how that even works, and if he can control his travelling, what is to stop him from travelling to my home?

Just reliving these thoughts I had is exhausting!

After my brain had a spasm from my internal question overload, I simply became worried that there was no way we would be able to find each other in a place like this, if he was here. The beach, walking path, and shops stretched for miles, far beyond what I could see, and there was no shortage of people.

I didn't have to worry for long. I decided I would just randomly pick a direction and start walking. I decided to choose the opposite direction I was facing. When I turned around, there he was, walking towards me. My heart skipped several beats, and my worry was quickly washed away by his smile. He was smiling! That was a good sign. He can't be that upset with me if he is smiling, right? And what a smile it is. He has to be at least six feet in height, but more like six-foot-one or six-foot-two. He was wearing blue shorts with a casual white button-down shirt, with a few buttons left undone. His hair was wavy but managed, with a rebellious piece hanging down in front, which drew attention to his dark eyes. It didn't suck watching him walk toward me. I swear, it's like someone dived into my subconscious, sneaked into all my dreams, and conjured up what I would perceive the perfect guy would be.

"Hey Stranger, I finally found you!" he said while handing me an ice cream cone. "I hope this flavour is ok."

I was so distracted by his smile, and overall good looks, that I completely failed to see that he was holding two ice cream cones until he offered one to me.

"This is actually pretty perfect, thank you!" It was two scoops of strawberry ice cream, in a waffle cone. My favourite.

"Shall we walk, or would you prefer to sit?" He gestured towards an empty bench.

"Walking sounds good." I nervously replied.

We started walking in the direction he just came from. I was the first to break the silence this time.

"How did you know I was coming? And to be waiting with ice cream. How did you know when I would come, so it wouldn't melt?"

"I actually got here after you," he explained. "I finally felt you and travelled here right away. I couldn't have arrived more than a minute after you. I noticed it was taking you a while to take in your surroundings, so I figured I had time to get us a snack." He said so matter-of-factly.

I felt embarrassed and he sensed that right away.

"You don't need to be embarrassed. I didn't want to disturb or startle you until you were in the right frame of mind. It's actually pretty cute to watch."

Cute? He thinks I'm cute! Or how I act is cute. Either way, I'll take it. It didn't help my nerves though. I don't feel extreme temperatures when I travel, but my palms were starting to feel sweaty. So gross.

"So, it has been a while," he said casually, to change the subject, and to maybe ask for an explanation, without sounding pushy.

"Yes, and I'm so sorry" I started to say, but he interrupted me.

"No, I'm sorry. I promised I would see you again, but I haven't been able to keep that promise. I was certain I would be able to know when you were travelling, but I haven't sensed you, until today."

"So the ice cream was meant to be a bribe?" I joked. "A distraction? Trying to keep my mind off how long it's been?"

"Well, more like an apology. Why did it work? Do you accept?" There was that smile again.

"Absolutely not, try harder." I tried to say this with a straight face, but failed. "Seriously though, it really isn't your fault, it's mine."

Before he could interrupt me, to try to further take some of the blame, I explained that this was the first time I had travelled since our last meeting. He was surprised to hear this because I had explained to him before how often I usually travelled, and to wait over half a year was very unusual.

I decided to tell him everything. How my parents have never fully embraced my ability, and how it changed our entire life. I then explained what I suspected my parents were doing, and my experiment to see if I was right. He agreed that it was unlikely that the pills were vitamins, but he didn't take my side about seeing it as a betrayal, or deception. He argued that my parents were just doing what they thought was right, and besides stopping me from travelling, my health did greatly improve, so it maybe shouldn't be seen as a deception but more of a misguided act.

Honestly, how dare he be so mature about this!

We debated back and forth a bit on this. I tried to further explain my side, and how I feel like I am treated as a prisoner in my own home, being punished for my gift. He only saw the love my parents have for me and understood how they just are trying to keep me safe.

I became kind of pissed at him.
I was close to leaving him, turning around and walking the other way, but I decided to stay. We walked in silence for a while.

"You don't like that I am not agreeing with you." He could see that I was agitated with him.

I decided not to respond because everything that wanted to come out of my mouth was either sarcastic or mean.

After a few more minutes, he tried to talk to me again. "I'm sorry I upset you, or made you angry. Something you need to know about me is that I never tell people what they want to hear. It clearly gets me into a lot of arguments, but you will always know exactly what I think, or where I stand."

"I just thought that you would get it." I bit back.

"I never said I didn't get it. I understand how you feel and why you feel that way, and I am on your side. I would love nothing more than to hear that you get a bit more freedom, or that your parents finally accept that your ability is a part of you, and not to be seen as a burden. I'm just saying that I can also understand their side of it all. It can't be easy watching your kid travel on their own since they were young, to distant places without their supervision. They are scared, for your safety and your health. Saying that, parents can also make mistakes."

"So you do agree that they should not have lied about the medication," I asked cautiously.

"Yeah, of course. You should know what you are taking, and if there is a choice about it, you should be in on the decision-making. Do you even know that they lied though?"

"What do you mean? Of course they lied!" Was he for real? "I'm standing here, with you right now, that shows me they lied!"

"You may be right, and your evidence against them is strong. I'm just saying, maybe when you get back, you might want to have a talk with your parents about it."

Ok, so he wasn't wrong. Maybe I have been a little selfish about everything. I have been more concerned about how I feel, and what was happening to me lately, than how it has been affecting everyone around me. Even Lotus has felt a little off whenever we talked, but I have never taken the time to ask her why. I didn't even tell her about my experiment, because she has also seemed happier the past six months. Plus, lately, she has been telling me to cut my parents some slack, which is not what I have been wanting to hear from her.

"I'm a brat." The words escaped my lips after my internal monologue came to an end.

"Not at all," he reassured me, accompanied with a little poke from his elbow, and a smile. "We just sometimes forget to see the other side sometimes."

"Are you even real? Or are you actually my conscience manifested into a form that I would finally pay attention to?" This was me attempting to flirt now. I know, I went from being pissed off to flirting so fast, that even I am impressed.

"As flattering as that sounds, I'm afraid I'm just a normal guy, but admittedly, I am trying to keep your attention."

My mind was screaming, 'Is this flirting?? Are we actually flirting now?'

I have no experience with boys. I am not smooth or cool. The only response my mind and body could come up with to his witty comeback was to giggle, and, wait for it, snort a little.

"Oh god!" I gasped in horror at my rookie mistake. I'm pretty sure rule number one on most flirting do's and don't lists is to refrain from snorting.

If the tension was starting to ease off, my little misstep helped erase it completely. He didn't run away like I half expected him to. Instead, he laughed and took my hand in his as we kept walking.

My inner monologue completely fangirled at this moment.

'His hand is so large but soft, and I am holding it! Or he is holding mine. Our fingers are laced, so I guess we are holding each other. Wait, I snorted, and he took my hand? Is his world opposite from ours? Is being dorky and uncool attractive there? Wait, would that make him like a nerd there? A freakin' hot nerd. Is my palm still sweaty? Does he think my hand is gross? How many hands has he held? Should I say something?'

He must have either sensed my mind going crazy or my face betrayed my inner thoughts. He asked "Is this ok?" while lightly squeezing my hand.

"What? Oh, this? Um, yeah, yeah of course. So ok!" Honestly, words kept falling out of my mouth. Finally, I stopped talking and just smiled at him. In return, he gave me a smile back, and if I wasn't mistaken, he was a bit nervous too. At that point, we both seemed to relax a little and kept walking.

"I just want to put it out there that if I disappear, I'm really sorry. I just have a feeling that I may not have that much time here today because the meds are still a bit in my system." I was already regretting that I had already wasted so much time by arguing with him.

"Then we need to make the most of our time together. If you're up to it, I would love to see exactly how far this beach goes. Doesn't it seem endless to you?"

I answered that I had that feeling about the beach too, and then we were in full, non-stop conversation mode. I asked him how the rest of the year was for him, and he went into detail about his travels. There were so many, and he admitted he travelled so much because he was looking for me. My side of the conversation was a bit more boring, as I explained the school work I caught up on, the books I had read, and the shows and movies I binge-watched. As boring as I thought it was, he seemed to hang onto every word and asked a lot of questions.

I decided not to ask anything too personal this time. After our meeting had such a rocky start, I wanted the rest of our time to be light and fun, and maybe even more flirty.

I have no idea how long we talked. The conversation was easy and constant, and without feeling any fatigue, we could have been walking for days. At one point, we concluded that the beach was endless and that the sun never set. We decided we should walk away from the beach to see what was beyond the shops, when I felt a small bit of nausea.

"I think our time is coming to an end," I said regretfully.

"Can I take you on a date?" That was not what I was expecting him to say.

"Yes, but how?" How do you date someone who you are not sure when or if you will see them again?

"The next time I find you, we will make it our official first date," he answered, like it was so simple.

"And if we end up someplace crazy, like on a scary erupting volcano?" I answered back, playfully.

"Then we will have the best first date story ever, won't we?" He was not wrong.

"Then it's a date," I said, afraid my face was going to break from the huge smile I couldn't wipe off. "But, what if I am not able to travel again for a long time, or you miss me the next time I travel?"

"I won't miss you again. I definitely have a lock on you now. That sounds a bit creepy, doesn't it?" He laughed nervously, and I made a mental note to ask him to fully explain this one day.

"Ok, but again, if I can't leave for months?"

"I'll wait for you."

He lifted my hand to his mouth, and then I was gone.

SAND

Tell me if this doesn't sound familiar. You plan a trip to the beach with friends or family. It's all you can think about for days until the actual day arrives. You pick out the perfect swimsuit, pack the perfect snacks, bring your favourite thirst-quenching drinks, and all your favourite beach toys. You have had everything planned and packed for days. You get there and have the best carefree fun, and enjoy some sun-soaked relaxation. The only consequence you can think of, or worry about, is getting a sunburn, but you even brought lotion to prevent that, if you remember to apply it.

But the day inevitably comes to an end. You pack up, give the beach one last look, and you reluctantly go home. It's when you get home, no, it's actually when you are in the car on the way home that you realised that despite all your perfect planning and packing, the memories of your amazing day at the beach will be, at least temporarily, overshadowed by all the freakin' sand you will be finding in everything for the next few weeks.

This is my life right now. I'm in a constant state of cleaning up sand, when all I want to do is reminisce about my walk on the beach with a cute guy.

GAH!

I'll explain.

I came home to chaos.

After Mom held on to me for dear life and Dad ran his tests, they finally told me that I was away for almost three days. To me, that was nothing. Really, it's one of the shortest times I have been away in a long time. But by the way, they were acting, you would think that I have been away for years.

Like my last trip, I came back exhausted, so I slept for most of the day. I arrived home sometime in the morning and slept until early evening. I was relieved to see that I didn't miss dinner. I was starving, but also wanted to have a nice family dinner. We sat down to eat, but no one said anything. It was awkward. Dad just kept his head down, and Mom looked like she was trying her best not to burst into tears. Reading the room, I decided it was best to just follow suit and keep my mouth shut.

The next morning, I assumed after breakfast my parents would be ready to hear about my trip, if we followed our usual timeline. We ate breakfast together, in almost silence. Mom didn't look like she was holding back tears anymore, but you could tell she spent most of the night crying. Dad gave me a few smiles, but they felt like sympathy smiles, or something else that I couldn't put my finger on. When they gave me my morning "vitamin," they were both watching me with great interest, so I knew I wouldn't be able to spit it back out. Taking one pill won't hurt. I had to take a few and I was still able to travel. I am hoping they ease off and I can get back to my fake-out routine. I do have a first date to look forward to!

After breakfast, I sat around waiting for them to

take me into the living room, where they let me tell my stories. It didn't happen, so I figured they weren't ready. On my way back to my room, I heard my parents talking in whispers. I tried to listen in but I couldn't make out what they were saying.

I didn't have to wonder for long what they were talking about, because within an hour my parents had me shower, pack a bag and we were in the car on the way to the city.

This was not a fun trip. It was straight to the hospital. I was poked by too many needles, inserted into every machine, hooked up to more machines, and I swear I saw every single doctor who worked in the city. They even made me talk to a psychologist AND psychiatrist. I saw these two every day. I was in the hospital for two weeks.

The worst part was, no one was telling me anything. Why was I being tested? What were they testing for? Why do I have to stay for so long, even though I felt fine? Admittedly, I was a bit weak and still tired, but fine nonetheless. I felt like I was going crazy. Seeing the "head doctors" just made this feeling worse.

The only thing that kept me sane these weeks was my visits with Lotus. She was allowed to come almost every day. When she visited, it was the only time my parents left me alone, so it was a double bonus. She brought me magazines, and snacks, and kept me updated with her social life. (She broke up with her girlfriend, after she caught her sending selfies to someone else, and was now starting to hang out with a guy she met at the mall. I love her life!) We also started to talk about our upcoming birthdays. We are both turning eighteen soon. I would love to do something special. Not a sleepover special, but something that involves leaving the house. I noticed Lotus got a little emotional when I brought up our birthdays. She waved it off and blamed the emotions on her period, so I let it go.

Lotus was the only one who cared to hear where I last went to (The head doctors asked but I felt they were just humouring me to appear friendly and gain my trust), so I told her about my day at the beach with Gabe. She said she was excited for me about my upcoming first date, which I thought she would be, but I didn't feel the enthusiasm. I was finally going to tell her about my experiment and what I suspected my parents had done/are doing, but she wasn't as outraged as I was about being forced to stay in the hospital, so I decided I would wait to explain it all to her.

"I mean, your Dad is a doctor, so he probably does know what's best for you. And if other doctors also agree with him, and just want to make sure you are ok, being here isn't such a bad thing."

"You sound like Gabe," I replied. "He has been trying to get me to see my parents' side of everything too."

"You mean, Gabe sounds like me! Sounds like a smart guy." Lotus laughed.

I am home now. I have been home for a few days. Because I was in the hospital for so long, I had to wait until now to write my last two entries. I have been so afraid that I would forget some details about the beach, or forget something Gabe said.

Dad brought a bit more equipment home from the hospital. I don't really know what to say about that. I don't really want to think about that.

Mom is hovering a lot again. Dad's moods have

shifted and he is back to looking worried and tired all the time. I guess you can say, it's business as usual again. The last six-ish months were a nice break, but this feels a bit more real.

I'M A NORMAL
TEENAGER!

It has been two weeks since my hospital stay, which makes it four weeks since I last travelled. Four weeks since I last saw Gabe.

Gabe and Lotus's feelings about my parents have been echoing a lot in my mind. I get what they are saying. I know when it comes to my ability, I need to be more empathetic, and a little less selfish when discussing it with my parents. I will acknowledge that I often dismiss how they feel about it, because I am so wrapped up in my adventures and experiences.

Am I being different from any other teenager though?

So I am a little boy crazy right now. Gabe may be what I most think about every waking minute of the day, but aren't most girls or boys my age acting or feeling the same way about someone they like? The only difference is that they have the opportunity to see their crush more often than I do. Perhaps I wouldn't be so boy crazy if I haven't been locked up and isolated since I was nine freakin' years old, and was allowed to socialise, attend dances, or even go on a few awkward dates. You can't deprive me of my teen years, and not expect me to enjoy the benefits of my ability, that little taste of freedom that I get when I travel.

I understand that my parents are worried about my safety, and about so many other unknowns. I get it, I do, but I'm turning eighteen soon. They have to let go at some point. I'm sure it is scary for any parent to let their kid leave, to become who they are going to be, to make their mark on the world. My situation really isn't that much different. If anything, it should be easier for them to let me go, they have been doing it for years.

I feel like they have never once tried to see things my way, just as I have been accused of not seeing their side. Can we not come together and find some middle ground?

So, that was the plan. I was going to demand an audience with my parents, and have a mature conversation about this. I would do my best to leave out the "my life isn't fair sentiments," and ask if we can come to some sort of compromise. I want to be more sympathetic to how they feel, and I would like it if they would stop treating my travelling as a death sentence. Maybe, in time, they can learn to feel a bit of the joy I feel about my ability. If it goes well, I might even bring up what I suspect about the vitamins. It would be a relief to get it all out in the open and to be involved in the conversation about what medications I should be taking.

Yesterday I decided that at breakfast, I would ask my parents to set aside a time that was convenient for both of them, so we could have a family discussion. I was really looking forward to this, and thought it would help solve a lot of problems.

When I was just outside the kitchen, I heard my parents talking in hushed tones. They didn't hear me approach, so I hovered just outside the doorway, hoping I could hear what they were saying.

I heard everything.

Mom: "OK fine, I am being emotional, but that doesn't mean I'm making my decisions based on my emotions. I have always worked from facts, you know this, so stop making me sound weak."

Dad: "OK, so we double the dose, and then what? When she gets used to that dose, do we just keep adding more pills?"

Mom: "I'm not concerned about later, we can worry about the later when we have the present figured out, and right now, it is recommended that we double the dose. You even agreed with the doctors. Why are you fighting me on this?"

Dad: "Fine, but I want to tell her the truth."

Mom: "No, we can't. And even if we tried, you know she won't listen, Eric, she never does!"

Dad: "But you think she will believe that she needs to take double the vitamins every day, after we have already lied and said she was taking a *special blend*."

Mom: "She needs to take those pills. I don't care what she believes at this point. You can try the truth, but if that backfires, she won't even continue taking the one pill she takes now. You know I am right!"

Dad: "Are we being selfish?"

Mom: "I'm not having that conversation right now."

Dad: "We can't postpone her leaving forever."

Mom: "I can, and I will postpone her leaving for as long as I can!"

I couldn't believe what I was hearing. On one hand, I was relieved to finally get confirmation outside my experimentation, that I was being given something other than a vitamin. My relief quickly turned to anger. How could they do that to me? Now they want to give me double the amount? My mom even admitted she is trying everything she can to prevent me from travelling.

I didn't enter the kitchen yesterday and stayed in my room for the remaining meal times. I told them I was in a mood and could make my own food. Mom showed up at my door with a muffin and pill and watched as I took it. There was only one pill, so I guess they are still fighting about how to proceed with lying to me. I managed to hide the pill in my cheek and spit it out when she was gone.

I was hoping we could all be mature about this, and discuss everything together, but when the adults are the ones being sketchy and deceptive, why should I be the mature one? So screw it! Experiment number two is officially underway.

Experiment Number Two

Title

The Power of Fatigue

Background

At the conclusion of my last experiment, (See previous journal entry "The Experiment") I was finally able to travel, after a night of movie bingeing, specifically the Twilight series. Since then, I have wondered if solely skipping the meds helped me travel, or if there are other variables I should consider to help me travel, helping me gain a little control over my ability.

Aim

I am going to test if being exhausted has a direct effect on my travelling.

Hypothesis

I am predicting that if I keep my body in an exhausted state, it will allow me to travel.

Risk Assessment

My health

- My overall health may decline. When I'm tired for a long period of time, I always get sick.

Parents

- I just want to note that I don't care how they will feel about this at this time.

Method

I am still going to try to avoid taking the deceptive medication my parents force me to take daily. It may prove more difficult because they are fighting about doubling the dose, so I need to figure out how to fake taking two pills. For now, I will stick to my hide-in-cheek, spit-it-out in a napkin approach.

Whether I am successful or not with avoiding the meds, I plan to only get four hours of sleep each night. I will stay up as late as I can without being detected. Specifically, I plan to stay up until at least three a.m. every night. I will set my alarm for seven a.m. the following morning. On the nights my parents prevent me from staying up this late, I will set an alarm to wake up early, picking whatever time gives me approximately only four hours of sleep.

Results

The experiment ran for only two and a half weeks.

During this time, I did get sick from lack of sleep and became a bit weak.

Despite having the pills in my system, I was able to travel.

Discussion

Three days into the experiment my parents doubled the dose of the meds I take every morning. The lame excuse they gave me was that the manufacturer of the pill originally provided us with the wrong dosage, so I should have always been taking two. Let's see what excuse they come up with when they think two pills are ineffective. I was only able to hide one pill in my mouth and spit it out. So I underwent this experiment with more medication in my system.

My extreme exhaustion was able to offset the benefits of the medication. Even with more meds in my system, my health declined on very little sleep, as opposed to last time when it improved with fewer meds but a normal amount of sleep.

Conclusion

Let them pump me full of whatever medication they want. I found my golden ticket to Gabe.

FIRST DATE

Can you die from pure happiness?

I just had the most perfect first date. It seriously has to be the most perfect first date there has ever been, in the history of all perfect first dates. Did I mention it was perfect?

I can't stop smiling. No one can bring me down from this high, not even my parents, despite their efforts to bring me back to their depressing reality.

Dear Diary, I like a boy, and he likes me back.
Elizabeth + Gabe
Gabe + Elizabeth
Elizabeth♥Gabe

Ok, I'll stop acting twelve…for now. It's time to get to the good stuff anyway.

I'm still pretty pissed off with my parents, so when I felt the nausea wash over me, I just left. I had time to find them and tell them I was leaving, but I chose rebellion. Screw the man, and all that. ANARCHY, or whatever.

I arrived in what looked like a town square. The

town itself looked small and charming, like it was ripped out of one of your favourite TV shows or Hallmark Movies. The Gilmore Girls came to my mind, and I quickly looked around to see if Lorelai or Rory would make an appearance.

How cool would it be if my ability allowed me to travel into movies or shows? Anyway....

The town looked like your typical small-town tourist destination. The buildings were old, made of brick, but were maintained and pretty. At a quick glance, I saw a candy shop, an ice cream shop, various specialty clothing stores, a small market, and a bookstore. The streets were lined with mature trees, and street lanterns decorated with hanging plants.

The shops followed alongside a road that was a literal square. In the centre of the square was where I stood. A large grassy open space, which I assumed the town used for all their functions and celebrations. Tonight the town was gathering with families and couples setting up blankets or chairs in front of a large white screen. A community movie night!

The sun had started to set, bringing about that magical golden hour. It has to be one of my favourite moments each day. Everything was washed in a beautiful golden/pinkish colour. My first thought was wishing I could experience this with Gabe.

As if he could read my mind, at that moment he stepped into my eyeline and was walking toward me with a black and white plaid blanket and a picnic basket. I almost didn't notice what he was holding again, because his smile was so captivating. As he approached, my knees got weaker with every step he took. When he finally reached me, I thought my legs were going to give out, but

I managed to stay on my feet.

"Elizabeth." He greeted me, with his low, yet velvety voice.

"Gabe," I replied, trying not to sound too nervous.

"So it looks like our first date is a movie in the park. It's not a scary erupting volcano, but I think we can make it work."

"Yeah, I mean, if we have to." I giggled, thankfully snort-free.

"So, I think I found the perfect spot for us. I figured we could sit near the back, that way if the movie is boring, we can talk without disturbing anyone, but we are still close enough to see and hear if the movie turns out to be good. But, if you want to sit closer, that works for me too." He was a bit nervous. I could tell he added the last part about sitting closer as an afterthought because he didn't want to seem controlling. It was cute and appreciative.

"I like your first plan," I answered. "It sounds perfect, but we better grab a spot on the ground quickly, the square is filling up fast"

While he was spreading out the blanket we were about to sit on, the ice cream incident came to mind.

"Ok, how long was I standing this time, looking around like a total goofball?"

"I mean, not that long. Just long enough that I had time to arrive, find you, and gather this blanket and basket." He tried to answer me without smiling, but this clearly amused him.

"Greeeaaat." I was embarrassed. I just hope my mouth was closed. My parents catch me all the time staring at whatever with my mouth wide open. Dad always tries to throw food in it.

"I don't think anyone else noticed you, but me. Plus

I told you before, it's cute."

"Where did you find the blanket and basket?"

"I bought it," he said so plainly and without explanation.

"You bought it? Where did you get the money?"

"I found cash in my pocket. It happened at the beach too. I guess it's another mystery just like how our clothes change on their own. You look really nice, by the way."

"What?" I had no idea what I was wearing. I completely forgot to look. I was wearing jeans, and a slightly oversized grey knitted sweater with large grey buttons, with a black tank top underneath. Not bad. "Oh my outfit, thanks! I didn't pick this out myself, but it's something I probably would have. You look nice too."

I felt weird saying that. He always looked good, but this is the first time I think I told him out loud that he looked good. I hope he didn't think I said it only because he said it first. He was wearing dark blue jeans, a light grey shirt with a black jacket. He looked like he stepped out of a men's magazine.

"Should we see what's in the basket? I didn't have time to see what I was buying, I just grabbed one. Hopefully, there is something edible in here." He chuckled.

We were both pleasantly surprised. Inside the mystery basket, was a variety of cheese, meats, a small loaf of bread, olives, grapes, and a bottle of champagne. Real, alcoholic champagne. Either they have no age limit on drinking here, or they assumed Gabe was of age.

At that moment, I realized that I had never asked Gabe his age. I had always assumed he was my age.

"How old *are* you?" I blurted out

He looked at me amused because to him, this question came out of nowhere.

"It's just that where I am from, there is an age restriction on alcohol, and I just assumed you were my age, or maybe here the drinking laws are different." I backtracked, trying not to ramble too much.

"I'm nineteen," he answered.

"I'm seventeen, but will be eighteen in a couple of months."

"Is it ok that I am older?" He asked, sounding a bit concerned.

"Yes, it's ok," I assured him. "We are pretty much the same age. I was just curious. I'm assuming this is the kind of stuff you find out on a first date."

"I honestly wouldn't know, this is my first ever first date," he said shyly.

"SHUT UP!" I blurted out.

He looked at me confused, because why wouldn't he?

"I'm sorry!" I quickly chimed in. " I'm just shocked! This is actually *my* first ever first date, and here I am so nervous, thinking I have no idea what I am doing, assuming you do."

"I'm nervous too," he admitted. "We can stumble through this together."

As I write this, I am still thinking he can't be real, or he is lying to me. How can someone who is so brave, kind and considerate, who looks the way he does, never had a girlfriend or been on a date?I was dying to ask him this exact question, but I decided to leave it to a later time. I didn't want to push, and for him to admit he was nervous couldn't have been an easy thing to do. It wasn't for me, anyway.

I think the town was waiting for the night to become darker before they started the movie, so we used this time to talk and nibble on the food, and drink champagne.

Gabe admitted he was surprised that I had travelled so soon. He was hoping he would see me sooner than later, but was prepared for a lengthy wait. I told him my theory about exhaustion, how I thought it could trigger my travelling, and how it obviously worked. I decided not to tell him about my hospital stay, or what I overheard my parents say. I think he realised I was avoiding the topic of my parents, so he refrained from asking about them, as I tried not to bring them up too much. I think we both didn't want to get into an argument. He did bring up his concern for my health, with making myself exhausted, which I thought was sweet. I assured him I had everything under control.

As I talked, I noticed he listened with such intent, that it was almost unnerving. He never stopped smiling, and his eyes alternated between making eye contact and watching my mouth as if he couldn't wait for what I was going to say next.

Before the movie started, one of the event organisers welcomed everyone to the park, gave a few housekeeping rules, like where the garbage should go, and introduced the movie we were about to see. He mentioned it was last year's number one big blockbuster action movie, and everyone seemed excited to be able to watch it again. Everyone's enthusiasm was contagious, so we decided to watch the movie to see if it was any good, and then we would continue chatting afterward.

The movie was terrible. It was laugh-out-loud terrible.

Apparently what constitutes a good movie here, is way different than where Gabe and I are from. Bad acting, terrible stunts, and weird camera work. Honestly, name something that would make a movie awful, and this movie had it. We laughed so hard we were both wiping away tears. We definitely bonded further over this film. Halfway through, Gabe took my hand and held it for the rest of the movie. When the movie finally ended, we laughed about it for at least another half hour.

"How much time do you think you have left here?" Gabe suddenly asked.

"Honestly, I am not sure, I never am, but if I have to guess, probably not long," I answered, sadly. " I had some of the pills in my system at the beach, which turned out to be a short visit, so I am assuming that tonight would be no different, especially having to take more of the meds lately."

He looked like he wanted to ask about me taking more medication, but I told him that was a story for another time.

" A story for another date? Unless you just want to hang out and be friends."

"I would love to go on another date with you," I replied. This time I made sure to keep eye contact when I answered, to show how into the idea I was.

This would have been the most opportune time for our first kiss. We had stopped talking but kept looking at each other, with stupid grins on our faces, while sitting close, still holding hands. I think he felt it too, because his smile started to fade and his eyes kept wandering away from my eyes, down to my mouth. So naturally, I freak out internally and ruin the moment.

I jumped up, said something stupid about having

a leg cramp, and asked if he wanted to go for a walk. I thought he was going to be upset with me, but he chuckled and agreed that a walk would be nice.

We decided to do some window shopping and walked by some shops. We walked hand in hand, commenting on what we saw, and engaging in some light flirty banter.

I remember thinking to myself that I never wanted this night to end, when my travel companion, nausea, made an appearance.

We quickly started to say our goodbyes.

"Would it be ok if I hugged you goodbye?" he asked.

I nodded yes, too afraid to say anything, worried my voice would betray my emotions.

He pulled me in for a hug, wrapping his arms around me, and held me until I left.

He felt strong, yet gentle, warm, comforting, loving. He felt like home.

MOVING FORWARD

I expected my house to be a shit show when I got back, and I was not disappointed. It was business as usual, really. Mom's smothering, Dad's examination, with more machines now, followed by a lengthy nap. I slept for almost twenty-one hours. I should have known that I would be even more tired when I got home, having to be so fatigued to leave.

When I woke up, I learned that I was gone for only two days. This is looking like a good compromise. Hear me out. If they insist that I must keep this drug in my system, I can work with that, if I am still able to travel. I can deal with my trips being short if I get to leave more often. My shorter trips also mean a shorter absence for me here at home, so it really is a win for everyone.

I realise that I have to start taking some accountability for my health. I can't run on so little sleep forever. Moving forward, after I travel, I will catch up on my sleep, try to eat healthy balanced meals, and only try to spit out one of the fake vitamins, not both.

I am also going to try to work on my relationship with my parents, if I can bear it. I don't want to be mad at them forever. I am hoping to get to a place where I can finally have that conversation with them about the pills, so we can be more open and honest with each other. Fingers crossed.

Having only been back from my date for four days, I have decided to give myself a good two weeks before I try to travel again.

HOUSEKEEPING

I have spent the last two weeks trying to bring about as much positive change as I could.

I feel fantastic. I have been sleeping a solid eight hours or more a night. I am eating my fruits and vegetables. I have been doing a bit of weightlifting with Dad, which he thought was so fun, and I have been joining Mom on her walks.

They have not asked about my last two trips, so I decided not to bring up my travelling with them. It hurts a little that they don't want anything to do with that part of my life right now, but I am trying to look at the situation from their perspective. They may just need a time-out right now, so that is what I am giving them.

Thankfully I have Lotus who is still willing to, and wants to, hear my stories. I'll get back to her in a minute.

I was able to have a discussion with my parents about the future, without Mom bursting into tears, or me yelling or storming off. I forgot to write about this, but when I didn't go anywhere for seven months, I was not only able to complete my high school credits, but Mom had enrolled me in some distant college courses. Nothing crazy, just some level entry courses. One is History and the other is an English course. Anyway, everyone my age, my old classmates, have recently gotten accepted to a University or College and are preparing to move away from home at the end of summer. My parents are suggesting that I stay home, for now, and continue taking college courses at home. They admit they are worried about my health and safety. They also realise that I am turning eighteen, which allows me to make my own decisions about my health and living arrangements.

I sat pondering their offer for a few minutes. They looked like they were preparing for a fight, but honestly, I thought it was a perfect plan, and to their relief, told them just that. I am planning on travelling more, if I can gain some control over it, so going to an actual college or trying to get a job would be difficult. I know I can't rely on my parents and stay at home forever, but for now, it would be nice to have this stability while I experiment with my ability.

Last night I was able to video chat with Lotus. I told her my college plans and she agreed that it was probably the best idea. She then told me all her plans.

She had received acceptance letters to every University she applied for, which didn't surprise me, but surprisingly chose to stay in the city, going to the University closest to home. It is actually one of the top Universities in the province, if not the country, but I just thought she would want to move away, like most kids want to do after high school. She explained that when your parents already give you all the freedom you could ever want, it doesn't become a priority when choosing where to go to school. Makes sense. She eventually wants to become a lawyer and has been emailing back and forth with my mom about it.

She also updated me on her love life. She is still dating the mall guy, but is keeping it casual. She wants to keep her options open for University.

It was then my turn to tell her about my first date with Gabe, and at her request, I made sure not to leave out any details. She agreed that it was a perfect first date, and thought I deserved it, since I had waited so long for this experience.

In my excitement to tell her about Gabe, I accidentally briefly mentioned how I was able to travel, despite the pills. I forgot that I didn't tell her about the fake vitamins or about any of my experiments.

CRAP!

So I had no choice but to tell her everything. She was angry with me, and honestly, I don't blame her. We did promise to never keep secrets, and this was a huge violation of trust. I told her my selfish reasons why I kept it to myself, basically, because I thought she was on my parents' side. She explained that she wasn't on anyone's side and was just worried about my health. I don't know why I didn't think of that.

Yes, I do. I was selfish. I am selfish. I have been so wrapped up with finally having my turn to experience normal teenage things, that it has made me a bad friend.

I told her my plans to better my health, and my relationship with my parents, to prove that I am trying to change. She reluctantly accepted my apology, after much grovelling, and we ended our call by renewing our promise to each other...again.

It felt so good to tell Lotus everything. I didn't realise how heavy a burden keeping all that from her had become. My parents will be next. I will get there with them, but not now.

Tonight I start my preparations for my next trip.

WISHING ON
A STAR

I just got home from my second date with Gabe. It looks like it is still the middle of the night. My parents don't know that I am back yet, and I would like to keep it that way for as long as I can. I just don't want to wait to write about this last trip. I don't want to forget any details.

It only took three days to travel after I started my fatigue prep.

I arrived in another field. It was dark, and it must have been for some time, because there was no indication that the sun had recently set, or that it would rise anytime soon. The full moon high above assured me of that.

I was not alone. I would say there were a few hundred people scattered about. Kids were running around, holding lanterns, and sparklers. Couples were making themselves cozy on the ground with chairs or blankets. A few groups had radios on, with music I had never heard before. Some groups were drinking, others had food. It clearly wasn't an organised event put on by a group or town, but everyone seemed to be gathered here for the same reason. Anticipation was heavy in the air, and I couldn't help but feel the excitement that was radiating off everyone who passed by.

After I had taken a few steps, I realised that we were not just standing in a field, but that the field gave way to a cliff. We were overlooking a large body of water that stretched out far beyond what we could see. The night was cloudless, and there was very little wind, so the water was calm and reflective. The view of the moon and stars over the water was enough to make this trip worthwhile, but I knew there had to be another reason why everyone was gathered. People were starting to calm down and pick a spot on the cliff to settle, all facing out towards the water.

"Maybe there will be fireworks" I mumbled to myself. Who doesn't love a good fireworks show, and it would be cool to see if this version of Earth made them differently.

"Actually, I overheard that we are in for a meteor shower." Said a deep voice behind me, almost in a whisper.

I had chills. The good kind.

I turned around to what was fast becoming my favourite smile. I have been craving seeing that smile again, going through withdrawal the last few weeks. It is difficult because we have not figured out how to bring back objects from our trips, so having a picture of each other is not an option yet.

"Hey, you." That was all I could think to say. Apparently, my brain was still on its way.

"Hey," he said back, while taking me into his arms for a hug hello.

Surprisingly, by the time he let go, my brain returned and I was able to say something with a little more substance.

"Tell me more about this meteor shower."

"I'm afraid I don't know much. On my way to find you, I overheard different people talking about a meteor shower, and how this year is forecasted to be better than the last few years. I'm assuming it is a yearly event." He explained.

"I have always wanted to see a meteor shower. Every time one is announced back home, it is either too cloudy to see anything, or I might see one shooting star, which you can't begin to call a shower."

"Did you at least make a wish when you saw your shooting star?" He asked.

"Actually, no. I always remembered when it was too late."

"Maybe we will remember to make one tonight." He said, as he grabbed my hand and led me through the crowd to look for a spot for us to watch the event.

I don't think there would have been a bad spot to choose. The field and cliff was long, or wide. I don't know, depending on how you look at it. My point is that everyone had an opportunity to have an unimpeded view that looked over the water.

Gabe managed to find a boulder that we could lean against.

"I don't have anything for us to sit on, but if you want, you can sit on my jacket." Gabe offered.

"Thanks, but I am ok with sitting on the ground" I assured him.

The offer of his jacket reminded me to look down to see if my clothes had changed. They did. I was wearing a pair of olive green hiking pants and a black zip-up hoodie with a white shirt underneath. He was wearing a pair of grey cargo-type hiking pants, a dark blue hoodie, and a light black jacket.

"I'm not exactly dressed for a date, am I?" I said after I studied our outfits.

"But you are. You are dressed for the activity we are doing, isn't that what matters?" He assured me. "You look beautiful to me. You could be wearing a plastic bag though, and I would still think you are the most beautiful here. You might get weird looks from everyone else though." He laughed.

"Luckily, your opinion is the only one that matters. I don't care what anyone else thinks, though, to be honest, since you got here, I completely forgot there was anyone else here." I was so proud of myself when that came out of my mouth. Look at me, stepping up my flirt game!

My boldness may have caught him off guard. He stared at me for a minute, with a goofy cute smile on his face, then shook his head, as if to come back to reality, or to find his words again. I will be honest, it was a bit empowering having this effect on him.

"I think to get up here, you have to do a bit of hiking. I didn't see any type of vehicles or even bikes." As he offered this explanation, his voice cracked a little. I could never have guessed that his deep, soothing voice was capable of that.

"That makes sense." I offered. "I wonder when this thing is supposed to start?"

"Maybe we should be watching already, to see if we can catch a shooting star here or there," he suggested.

As we both looked up, so we wouldn't miss a star, the sky suddenly filled with hundreds of lights that streaked across the sky. It was the most amazing thing I have ever seen in my life. I just don't have the proper words to describe how awesome this was. When it started, everyone turned off their lights and radios, so we could all truly enjoy this pure wonder.

The meteors didn't stop. The sky showed no signs of a beginning or end to this miraculous phenomenon. It actually overwhelmed me with emotion, and I think it did the same to Gabe. He pulled me in close, put his arms around me, and I laid my head on his shoulder as we watched.

"Is this ok?" He whispered to me.

"Yes," I said breathlessly. "This is perfect."

We watched the lit-up sky for a while. I honestly couldn't tell you for how long. I felt like Gabe and I were in a bubble where time stood still, yet time moved on outside of us.

I felt him shift, so I immediately sat up, not wanting to cause him discomfort.

"Am I hurting you?" I asked.

"No, not at all, I just wanted to look at you...and maybe ask you something." He looked and sounded nervous.

"Is everything ok?" Of course, my brain immediately thought something was wrong.

He grabbed my hand. We were still sitting close together.

"What? Oh, everything is good. It's just...." He trailed off.

I decided not to say anything, fearing I would say the wrong thing, and discourage him from asking what he wanted.

"I was, uh...can I kiss you?"

My heart skipped all the beats, and my head felt tingly and hot. I was too nervous to even ramble, so like our first hug, I slowly nodded yes.

As he moved his face closer to mine (I didn't move, I was paralyzed with anticipation), I noticed his breathing became a bit heavy. I quickly checked mine, and found it had matched his. I felt like if he didn't kiss me soon, I was going to start hyperventilating, not that I wanted to speed up this moment. You only get one first kiss.

When he was close enough for our noses to almost touch, his hand, the one that wasn't holding mine, came up and his forefinger and thumb rested ever so softly under my chin. I chose this moment to close my eyes, and instinctively my lips slightly parted while I waited.

I felt his hot breath before I felt his lips. His lips were softer than what I had imagined, because really, I had no clue what it was really like to kiss someone. When I felt them, my lips met his, like they knew what to do.

I was so thankful we were sitting down because my legs started shaking, and I would have fallen. I always thought the phrase 'weak in the knees' was a metaphor for something or just a saying, but it is an honest, true reaction.

Our first kiss was brief. He moved back slightly so he could look at me, to make sure I was ok, and probably to see if I liked it. I was also wondering if he liked it too. When we opened our eyes, we both had a smile on our faces which told each other that we did like it. He leaned in and kissed me again, and we didn't stop kissing until the meteor shower ended.

I didn't know if he had ever kissed another person before. If I was his first date, this could also be his first kiss. Our kisses were slow and soft. It's like we were both learning as we went, experimenting with how to tilt our heads, how to move our lips, what pressure we should use, how wide we should open our mouths, and how and when to use our tongues. It didn't take us long to get the hang of it and to become attuned to each other.

Our kissing time bubble burst when we heard people talking and laughing and walking about. The meteor shower had ended, and everyone was packing up to trek down the hill to go home. We looked at each other and started to laugh. It was an "Oops, we missed most of the event, but we finally kissed and would miss it all over again" type of laugh. At least, that is how I interpreted it.

"Was that your first kiss?" he asked.

"Yes, was it that obvious?" I joked.

"No, no! I wasn't asking ....I mean...It was mine, so I was just curious if it was yours. I promise I didn't mean anything bad."

"I'm sorry, I shouldn't joke. I guess I was only half joking, and half insecure, wondering if it was ok, because yes, that was my first kiss." I told him.

"Oh my god, it was more than ok. Honestly, I want to keep going, but I'm afraid you are going to slip away soon, so I wanted the chance to talk before that happened," he admitted.

"I too think this might be a short visit, but it's ok. I think I am really on to something, and have figured out how to trigger my travelling. It's not the same control you have, but it is better than leaving it to chance."

He knew about my exhaustion tactic from my explaining it on our first date and had already voiced his concern for my health. I explained how I plan to make my health a priority when I am home and will give myself a few weeks in between each trip to recuperate and build up my strength. He agreed that was a good plan and liked the idea of seeing me more often, even if the trips were short. Waiting two to three weeks and seeing each other for a few hours was better than waiting months at a time, even if we got an entire day or two to be together.

"Would you like to spend my birthday with me?" I surprised myself with this question. It just came rushing out of my mouth.

"Really? You want to spend it with me?"

"It is just over a month away. I can't guarantee I will be able to travel on that exact day, but I want to try. It will probably be my next trip."

"What about your parents or Lotus? Turning eighteen is a pretty big birthday, don't you want to spend it with them as well?"

"Ideally, I would love to spend it with all of you together, but since that can't happen, I would like to do something different this year. Every birthday is the same. I am either stuck at my house, or I'm stuck at Lotus's. I'm never allowed to go out. I want adventure, I want fun, I want something special, I want you." Look at me, I kiss a guy and become this bold, courageous woman who isn't afraid to say what she wants.

He didn't answer right away, but chose to kiss me instead. When he finally pulled away, he said "Of course I want to spend your birthday with you. I would be honoured."

That was when my body told me we had to say our goodbyes. He gave me one last kiss, and held me until I left.

BIRTHDAY PREP

I t has been three weeks since my last entry. I don't think I need to write about what happened when I last got home. It was the same old drill.

Lotus and I got into a fight last night.

Let me backtrack. I am still planning to try to travel on my Birthday, or as close to the day as I can. I really want to spend my day with Gabe. My plans solidified when my parents told me that for my birthday, I could either have Lotus come for a sleepover here, or I could spend the weekend at her house again. I'm turning freakin' eighteen years old. I am done with sleepovers. Let me go to a nice restaurant, or an amusement park, or do what everyone else my age is doing, trying to get into clubs.

I was debating whether to tell my parents my plan or not, but I realised doing so would force me to explain how I would be able to leave when I wanted. I would have to tell them everything, and I am still not ready for that yet. I am still finding it hard to justify telling them the truth, when they still haven't come clean with me about what they are doing.

The one person who I have to tell about my plan is Lotus. A promise is a promise, and I really don't want to disappoint her again. Plus, if she is planning anything special for me, I need to let her know that I won't be around.

My birthday is less than two weeks away, so I figured last night I should talk to her.

We text a lot, so I could have just texted, or even called, but this was an important conversation, so I thought a face-to-face video call would be appropriate.

We always start the call by Lotus updating me on her life. She didn't have much to report. Still casually seeing 'mall guy,' and has just been enjoying her last few months as a high school senior.

Senior prom is what everyone is talking about. Lotus has an idea to try to convince my parents to let me be her date. It is the last school dance she will ever go to, and she wants me to come as her plus one. I feel honoured and excited about the possibility of finally going to a dance with my best friend, but in my heart, I know it is not going to happen. I have stopped daring to hope. I didn't tell her that though. I don't think that counts as breaking our "truth promise."

We finally got to the reason why I asked for the call.

"I wanted you to know that I have decided to spend my birthday with Gabe." I had told her about our second date a few days after I got back, so I figured this wouldn't be much of a surprise, but I was wrong.

"What? But it's your eighteenth birthday! We have been talking about celebrating our eighteenth birthday together since we were little." She already sounded hurt.

"We can still celebrate it together, just not on the day" I assured her. "We have done that for a lot of our birthdays, it's no big deal."

"It is a big deal. It's a big milestone." She reminded

me.

"Exactly, it is a big milestone, and for once, I would like to do something special" I tried to explain.

"Being with your best friend isn't special enough?"

"That is not what I am saying. Please, don't take this personally. I love our sleepovers and look forward to them, but you have to see this from my point of view. I need to do something different. I have celebrated every milestone the same way."

"I see you choosing a guy over me and your family. I would never have done that to you!" She was angry.

"Seriously? You have never *had* to because I was never an option." Now I was getting angry.

"Don't you dare suggest that I would never choose you over others."

"But the reality is that I am not an option. You don't have to worry about scheduling dates around me, or worry if your other friends would get along with me, because I am just not in play anymore, and haven't been for a long time. I am someone who you only have to pencil in a few times a year. My parents have made sure of that." At this point, I could tell she was fighting back tears, but I needed to get my point across.

"Right now, I need you to be happy for me. I have, by some miracle, found someone who is like me, and I need to explore that. I finally have a chance to date someone and have a boyfriend. It's my time to finally have a bit of a life." I finished.

"I choose you every day. You are the first person I text when there is any news to share, when there is juicy gossip, or when I just find something funny. I tell you all my good and bad news before I tell anyone else. Just because I'm not able to physically be with you, it doesn't mean you are not an option to me."

"Lotus…I know…believe me….."

"No, Liz, you don't know" she cut me off. "It is always how bad shit it is for you. Poor Liz can't leave the house, poor Liz doesn't get to go to a dance, and poor Liz can't date. I get it, your life is restricted and it sucks, but it's not like there isn't a good reason for that. What you don't understand is that it's been hard for me too. I have had to spend the last nine years growing up with the person I care most about at arm's length. You were supposed to be there to meet and judge all the people I dated, go shopping with me every time I started to hate my clothes, get bad haircuts with me, see all the movies we like together in theatres, or go with me to all the lame school dances. I'm not constantly fighting your parents to let you go to a dance just for your benefit, it's for mine too." She cried.

"I'm so sorry Lo, I didn't realise."

"No, you didn't, no you don't. Look, I'm happy you have found someone, you know I am, but honestly, this isn't even about him. This might be the last birthday we get to celebrate together. Don't you understand that?"

"Lo, you are just going to University, and in the same city, it's not like we won't be able to see each other." Why is she being so dramatic? "I promise to be around for your birthday."

"Will you though? Do you know this? *Can* you know this?" She said super sarcastically. "Your parents told me to never bring this up, but I don't care. Every time you *leave* there is a chance you won't come back. Plus, you never *actually* know when you are going. Can you just for once open your eyes, come back to reality and see how things really are? My god, you are so in denial!"

"I'm sorry you feel this way, but my mind is made up. I'm not asking for your permission, I'm telling you what I have decided." I probably sounded a bit too harsh here, but at this point, I was just done. I wanted support but I just got a huge guilt trip.

There was an awkward silence for a few minutes. Lotus looked like she was unable to talk, and used this time to wipe away tears and clean up her eyes. I didn't know if I should say anything. Finally, she spoke.

"Liz, I love you, but when you get back from your '*trip,*' don't call me, I don't want to hear about it. At least, not for a while. I need time."

And then she hung up.

What the hell?

I'm still trying to process this. I thought she would be more than happy for me. She has had so many boyfriends and girlfriends that I have lost count, and I would spend hours on the phone with her talking and texting about each one. Not once did I ever make her feel like she couldn't talk to me about her love life, despite the fact that I was never allowed to have one. I have been a good friend. I have been selfless. Why is she being like this?

Honestly, screw everyone right now. For once, I am going to do something that I want, on my timetable. I have lived by everyone's strict rules and have been a captive long enough.

Prep for my Birthday trip starts in one week!

HAPPY BIRTHDAY TO ME!

D on't you love it when you plan something, and it actually works out like you intended?

On the morning of my eighteenth birthday, I was able to escape my boring, predictable, restrictive, beige life, to celebrate it with my boyfriend.

Yeah, I have a boyfriend now. It's official, no big deal.

I have been home for maybe a half hour. It's just after three in the morning, so everyone is asleep. I am being as quiet as I can, so they don't know I am home yet. It looks like I have been gone for ten days, if I am looking at the calendar right. That doesn't seem right though. I wasn't even gone for a full day, by my account. My parents are not going to be happy.

I left without saying goodbye again, but this time it really wasn't intentional. I woke up early, excited because I was finally eighteen, but more importantly, to keep myself from getting too much sleep. I don't want my parents to know how early I wake up, so I usually lay in bed for a few hours watching some shows or movies on my phone or laptop.

I was up for only an hour when my body told me I needed to prepare to go. My parents weren't awake, so I just lay in bed waiting to leave.

I arrived at what looked like a Renaissance or medieval fair. Except it turned out it wasn't like a modern-day fair you can visit, where everyone is dressed up, and you watch people play knights while you eat a deep-fried chocolate bar. To everyone around me, it was just a fair. Wherever I had landed, this was all real in their present timeline.

Immediately I looked down to see what I was wearing. I have always wanted to wear a Renaissance costume. I was wearing so many layers of clothing it was ridiculous.

I had on a long-sleeved, white undergown, its length went below my knees. Then over top, I had on a white corset-type top, that laced up in the front. Then there was a long flowy skirt that went over the white gown that went to my feet. This was a brownish colour. The colour of the skirt wasn't really important because a dress was fitted over top of everything else I was wearing. The dress was a deep red in colour, with long sleeves. It was long enough to cover the skirt that was under it. Like, the corset, the dress was also laced up in front. The corset and the top of the dress were tight, and it not only showed a little more cleavage than I was used to, but it also flattened my boobs and smooshed them high. So weird. My shoes were flat, made of leather from some kind of animal hide. My hair was simple, left down, wavy, and flowy.

Much like our modern fairs, there were booths set up for vendors to sell their goods. Food, clothing, jewellery, tools, animals, and drinks made up most of the booths.

At this point, I was closely looking at all the vendors to determine whether or not I had found myself in a larping situation, or if this was the real deal. The jury was still out. That was when I felt a tap on my shoulder. I turned around to find Gabe standing in front of me, smiling that smile that had become my drug of choice.

"Happy Birthday," he said, as he handed me a single long-stemmed red rose.

"Thank you, this is beautiful." I couldn't stop smelling the rose. It smelled so much better than our roses, or maybe it just smelled better because it was the first rose a guy has ever given me. Either way, I might have looked like a freak, as I kept sticking my nose in it, repeatedly, but luckily, Gabe was a gentleman and ignored my crazy behaviour.

"What do you think about having to spend your birthday here?" He took my hand and we started walking.

"Honestly, I think this is amazing! I'm wearing too many layers of clothing for my taste, but I'm excited to be here. Wait, let me look at you." I wanted to study his outfit. I was having too much fun playing dress up.

He had on dark brown pants that tucked into tall black boots that went up to just below his knees. He wore a puffy white, long-sleeved shirt, similar to my underdress, but his shirt had a collar. Overtop of the white shirt, he wore a sleeveless dark blue tunic, that laced up in the front. He wore a belt around his waist, not to keep his pants up, but designed to hold weapons. He had a long dagger tucked into the belt.

We both concluded after walking around for a bit that we were dressed as what we would consider the middle class. We definitely were not dressed as the rich were, but had on nicer clothing than others. We blended in nicely. The last thing we both wanted was to draw attention to ourselves while visiting, and if we were dressed as the noblemen and women, we definitely would have gotten a lot more looks.

"So, when I was walking around, looking for you, I overheard that there are several tournaments taking place today. Archery, sword fighting, and then, saved for last is the main event, the jousting tournament. Is that something that interests you? Or do you want to walk around some more to find something else to do?"

"I definitely want to check out the tournaments!" I answered enthusiastically. It felt like I had walked on the set of a Robin Hood movie. I wanted to see it all.

This is how we spent most of the day. All the tournaments were played out in the same arena. There was bleacher-type seating for the common people, like us, and the nobility had their own special seating area. We had really good seats and decided not to move, so we wouldn't lose our place. This was easy because we never got hungry, thirsty, or needed to find a bathroom on our trips.

Archery was my favourite tournament. Those who won, did so by pure talent and skill, instead of brute force and luck like the other events. I didn't expect the sword fighting and jousting to be as violent as they were. They didn't fight to the death, but there was more blood and injury than I cared for, but I still stayed to watch because I enjoyed the ceremonies. Just like some movies I have watched, the jousters were gathering favours from young pretty girls, promising them wins. I also enjoyed it when the underdog was able to claim victory.

While we watched, we were very aware that PDA might be frowned upon. We just didn't see anyone taking part in kissing or hugging their partners, so we discreetly held hands, but that was it.

When the tournaments were over, we decided to skip the rest of the festivities, for now. We wanted to be alone. A forest bordered the event grounds, and that was where we went. We found a beautiful old tree to sit under.

"I wish I could have gotten you a present," Gabe said as we settled ourselves under the tree.

"I love my rose," I assured him, as I smelled it again for the thousandth time.

"But you can't bring it home with you." He reminded me.

"No, I guess I can't." I sat for a minute just staring at my rose, when I got a bold idea. "There is something you can give me, that I can take back with me."

"Oh really? " He replied in a flirtatious tone. "Name it, and it's yours."

"Well…." I started, trying to dip into the courage that was there just a minute ago. "I have a question I want to ask."

"And my answer would be what you bring home?"

"Yeah…" I trailed off. I was chickening out.

"Elizabeth, you are killing me with suspense" he joked as he grabbed my hand, to further encourage me to speak.

"Are we…well, do you want to be…can we….um….boyfriend and girlfriend." I am a bumbling idiot.

He said nothing, but just smiled at me and laughed a little.

I felt dumb. I was about to say forget it, when he

interrupted me.

"I'm sorry, you are just really cute when you ramble. I know I should try to help you out when you do it, but I can't help myself but watch." He admitted.

"I'm glad my temporary brain malfunctions amuse you." I hate being made fun of, especially if it makes me feel stupid. I started to pull away.

"Elizabeth, I'm sorry. I promise I am not making fun of you. I mean it, you are really cute when you are nervous, and it makes me a dumb, awe-struck idiot. That is why I laughed. It's like when you see a puppy, and you get so overwhelmed by how adorable it is, you start laughing."

"So I'm a puppy to you?" I was calming down but remained slightly guarded.

"Actually, I was hoping to call you my girlfriend, if you still want that." Of course, he said this with that smile. A smile that could thaw the coldest of hearts.

"I guess that would be acceptable," I said this with a smile and an eye roll. This was me playing it cool.

He responded by pulling me in close and kissing me, and we didn't stop for hours.

I thought we had perfected kissing each other during our last date, but I quickly learned that there is always room for improvement. This time, we both gave permission to each other to allow each other's hands to explore more freely. That is all I am going to say about that.

We finally stopped our exploration, when we were running dangerously low on oxygen, or so it felt, and when we knew we had gone as far as we dared to go during our makeout session. By this time, the sun had set, and we found ourselves sitting in the dark.

We heard music in the distance, coming from the festival.

"As much as I want to keep you here, all to myself, maybe we should head back to the festivities. I don't want you to miss out on anything fun." He suggested.

I reluctantly agreed, and we walked back to the event grounds, hand in hand. When we got back to the festival, I was overjoyed to see that the night had progressed into live music and dancing around a large communal bonfire. Gabe and I spent the rest of the night tasting food and wine and dancing silly together.

Just as the sky started to hint that a new day was about to begin, my internal navigator told me that it was time to say goodbye.

This goodbye was hard. We both expressed how much we hated leaving each other just then, so I promised I would do my best to see him in two weeks time.

We kissed goodbye, and he held me until I left.

BOYFRIEND

It has been ten days since my last entry.

My parents were upset that I was not around for my birthday, but they were kind enough to celebrate it with me when I got back. My mom has been very emotional since my last trip. When my parents were singing 'Happy Birthday,' Mom barely got through it without crying.

I have made more of an effort to spend time with Mom in the last week. She won't tell me what is bothering her, but I can see that my spending time with her is helping her not feel so sad.

They still haven't been truthful with me, so I haven't told them anything either. I have given them many opportunities to tell me the truth, and have steered conversations in many directions to encourage it, but they still choose to avoid the topic.

In other news. I have a boyfriend, and I can't tell anyone, because no one wants to hear about it. My parents still won't entertain my travel stories, and Lotus still won't speak to me. She told me she needed time, but yesterday I couldn't take it anymore, and I texted her. I didn't know what to write, so I just reached out with a

"Hey" and a heart emoji. She ignored me.

I am starting my travel prep tonight to see Gabe. I am hoping to see him in two to three days.

Yesterday something came to mind when I was in the shower, as where all my deep thoughts come from. Gabe avoids talking about himself. Sure, he will talk for hours about his adventures and experiences but he is an expert when it comes to avoiding personal questions.

I had mentioned that before, in my previous Gabe findings, but somehow have forgotten to follow up on the unknown details, and unanswered questions.

I am trying to think back on our last few outings. I know after the beach, I have been wanting to keep the conversation light and fun. From the beginning, it was evident we were both attracted to each other, so I wanted to explore that and avoid further arguments. But now that we are dating, shouldn't our conversations become more personal?

I am compiling a list of questions that I am going to ask him, and demand answers to, when I see him next.

Where does he live?

How does his parents feel about his travelling? (And tell me about your parents.)

Do you have any siblings?

How are you able to know when and to where I travel?

Could you always control your ability, or is the control learned?

Is Gabe your real name?

NOT AMUSED

I have just arrived home. Luck is on my side, again, as it is just after four in the morning, so I have time to myself before my parents wake up, realise I am home, and I become a lab rat, then take my day-long nap.

I had an amazing time, and I will get to my day in a second, but first, what I should be doing, and want to be doing, is recording all the answers I finally discovered about my new boyfriend, but I have none. Zero answers. I honestly have no idea what happened.

I wrote down the questions and memorised them. I said them out loud for days, in the order that I wanted to ask them. I even practised what I would say if he gave me vague answers. I was going to tell Gabe as soon as I saw him that we needed to talk before we did anything. I had a plan, and was determined to see it through, so what the hell happened? It is like I was put under some sort of spell or something. I came home, smiling, missing Gabe, and had forgotten all about my mission until I picked up this journal and opened it to my last bookmarked page, where I had written out my questions.

So I guess I will retrace my steps to try to figure this out.

I arrived in a parking lot. A very large parking lot. The kind where you need to memorise a letter and a colour after you park, or risk losing your vehicle. The cars looked normal to me, like I could be on my Earth.

There really wasn't much to see, that is, until I looked up. Roller Coasters! I was at an amusement park! I haven't been to one since I was little, and at that time, I was too small to ride any of the good rides.

I immediately started walking towards what I assumed was the front gate. As I walked, I quickly checked on my outfit, to see if I was wearing something appropriate to spend the day on rides. I was wearing black workout leggings, black running shoes, a light grey t-shirt, and a dark grey sweater tied around my waist. Nice.

When I got to the gate, Gabe was there waiting for me. He held up two admission tickets and looked just as excited as I was to be there.

"Before we do anything, I want to have a talk. I need to have a talk, would that be ok?" I asked him right away, before he could speak and make plans.

"Yes, of course. I hope everything is ok?" he asked.

"Oh, it is, I just have a few things I really need to talk about," I assured him.

"Then we will talk, but I suggest we do it inside, so we are not in the way standing here at the entrance."

I agreed. He then kissed me hello, took my hand, and we entered the park.

That is the last time I can remember wanting to have a talk with him. I mean, we talked all day, but nothing close to what I wanted to talk about.

I remember we got through the gate and it was like my mind flipped a switch, and suddenly I had us running to line up for the first roller coaster I saw. He didn't try to prevent me from asking questions, or steer the conversation away from anything personal, I simply forgot what I was determined to do within seconds of entering this park.

When I look at it objectively now, it feels like the park itself was designed to keep me from thinking about anything serious. It was busy, with people everywhere you turned. The parking lot was huge and was almost completely full, yet each ride we went to had no lines. We never had to wait for anything. We never actually had a chance to just sit down and talk, because we never had to. We didn't get hungry or thirsty, so there was no need to actually sit down, but at the same time, whenever I thought it would be nice to have a sit-down and just be together, every restaurant, every picnic table, every bench was full. It felt like the day was programmed to keep me busy, happy and distracted.

When I say that out loud, it sounds crazy, I sound crazy. It's crazy, right? I never know where I am going to travel to, so it's not like this place was built just for me, to keep me busy, to distract me from asking my boyfriend questions. But maybe this place was built for the purpose of keeping everyone busy and distracted and perhaps I was led there? Wait, could he have somehow led me there?

He can control his travelling; maybe he can do more than just control himself. But that means, he could have purposely brought me to that village where they were killing all those people. Why would he do that though? What would be the point of that?

To gain my trust.

Did he place me in danger, so he could save me? He tells me that he arrives after me, but how do I know he is telling the truth? I have no way to check if this is true or not.

He just doesn't seem like the manipulative type. Or is that how manipulative people come across? He is kind, gentle, a good listener, and protective. He always makes sure I am in agreement with whatever activity we do and has always asked for consent when we are active in other ways. If there are any red flags, I am clearly blind.

Well, I guess if there are any red flags, the biggest one would be who the hell is he? But is it his fault I don't know? Again, he only dodged my questions that one time, then I decided not to ask, and now, I keep *forgetting* to ask, somehow.

I'm frustrated and confused.

As for the rest of the trip, we just went on rides until I had to go. He kissed me goodbye, we both wished I could stay, and he held me until I was gone.

Shit, I hear someone up. Here we go again.

BETRAYED

My best friend isn't talking to me, but apparently, she is talking to my parents.

What the F-

My parents just sat me down for a legit intervention. They even called it that! I'm sorry, but I'm not a drug addict, or an underaged alcoholic. This was extreme. If you want to have a discussion with me, that's fine, but to sit me down like I have done something wrong! Like I have a problem! This whole situation could have been avoided if my parents told the truth in the first place.

The worst part about this whole thing was that it was all Lotus's fault. She ratted me out! She completely betrayed my trust by telling my parents everything. She is still pissed off at me, so she reached out to my parents, saying she is worried about my health, but it feels like she just wanted to get back at me for choosing Gabe over her, for one freakin' day!

My parents sat me down, explained this was an intervention, and then said nothing, but handed me a printout of Lotus's email, asked me to read it, and then asked me to explain myself.

I'm gluing it to the next page.

Worried about Liz

Lotus Johnson

<Lotus_Love@yourmail.com>

June 10, 5:26 pm   (10 days ago)

Hi Gwendolyn,

Thank you for letting me know that Liz is gone again.

Forgive me for not calling, but this is difficult for me to bring forward, so I thought it would be easier to just write to you.

I'm sure by now that Liz has told you we had a fight and have not spoken since. What she probably didn't tell you was why we fought.

Everything I am about to tell you was told to me under the promise of secrecy. I know there is a chance I may lose Liz forever, but I am too worried about her to stay quiet.

First, she figured out a long time ago that the pills you are making her take every morning are not vitamins. She suspected they were something more when she was able to stay with us for over six months. She started hiding the pill in her cheek and spitting it out when you were not looking, to see if she would "travel" again with the drug out of her system.

Recently, she overheard you and Eric talking about the pills, and needing to double the dose. This gave her confirmation that she was right about the meds. She has been angry with you two. She feels that you should have had a discussion with her about the meds before she took them, or at least have come clean about deceiving her by now.

I think she has only been able to spit out one of the pills you give her every morning, so she is still taking at least one every day.

If you think the pills aren't working, it is because she has figured out a way to work around the pills. She has admitted to me that if she makes herself so tired, to the point of exhaustion, she can go on one of her *trips.*

I'm sorry I kept this from you. I know I should have brought this to you sooner, but you have to understand that she is my best friend and I didn't want to betray her trust. But now anyone can see that her health is declining fast, and I am so worried about her. How can she not see what we see when she looks in the mirror? Oh, and now she is seeing a guy? She says she is dating him, which is the reason why she is trying to leave so much. This is why we are fighting. She told me she was choosing to spend her birthday with him and was going to weaken herself to make this happen. I may have lost it on her, and told her I needed time away from her, but now I am afraid I'm running out of it.

I love her so much, but I am so frustrated with her. I just don't know what to do anymore.

Please let me know when she comes back.

Thanks,

Lotus.

"What do you want me to say?" I said after reading the email.

"Is it true?" Mom asked.

"Yes, all of it" I answered back, unemotionally.

"We aren't here to yell at you, We - "Dad started saying when he was interrupted.

"Why would you do this to yourself?" Mom blurted out.

"What your Mom means to say is that we are worried about you. You are purposely making yourself sick, and we are here to try to understand why."

"But you know why. Lotus explained it all in her email." What else did they want me to say?

"I just don't understand why you are trying to leave us?" Mom was trying to keep it together, but her voice was betraying her.

"I'm not trying to leave you, I'm trying to have a life, like every other person my age." Why is she making this about them?

"But you are not like everyone your age. And why the secrecy?" Mom asked.

"Ok, let's talk this through. Why have I been doing this behind your back? Why would I choose to keep this from you? Hmm...Gee, I wonder?" I may have overdone it with the sarcasm, but I was so mad, and I was also trying to keep it together, and not cry like a baby out of pure frustration.

"First, you just stopped caring about my trips." I started it.

"Oh, here we go again..." Mom interrupted me.

"Yes Mom, my trips. Whether you like it or not, I have been travelling since I was a kid. At least up until recently, you would let me tell you about where I had

173

been, but lately, you and Dad can't even pretend to care about this part of my life. You have always treated my ability like a burden, and won't even try to see the beauty in it."

"Eric, seriously, how many times do we..." Mom started to plead with Dad, but he stopped her from talking by shaking his head and giving her a pitiful smile.

"Then you lied about the drugs, then lied about them again when you thought they weren't working, and gave me more. Who does that? Honestly, I blame myself for believing that there was a *special blend* of vitamins made just for me. Saying that out loud now sounds so ridiculous."

"You're right," Dad admitted. "We shouldn't have lied to you about that. In our defence, you have always had a difficult time understanding why..."

"Why you hate it when I leave?" I finished for him.

"Well, yes, but not just that, Lizard, you -"

"Dad, I do get it. Both Lotus and Gabe have been trying to get me to think about how this affects you and Mom more, so I ..."

"Who the hell is Gabe?" Mom interrupted me.

I just want to say that as far as interventions go, this one sucked. Aren't we supposed to let everyone talk, without interruption?

"See, this is what I am talking about! Gabe is my boyfriend, Mom. You would know this if you actually cared about that part of my life. So yeah, I have figured out a way to see him more often. Has it been sneaky? Honestly, I don't think so. I would have told you about him and how I have been trying to control my ability, if we were all open and honest about everything. But if you insist that I have been secretive, then let's just call us even."

"So you are purposely trying to leave because you are seeing a boy," Dad said slowly.

"Eric, I thought I could do this, but I can't. This is just ridiculous. I think it's time that we -"

"Mom, one of these days, you will have to let me go! I'm already eighteen. I can't be locked up in this house forever!"

"You are right, the day is coming when I will have to say goodbye. I have accepted that, but I can't stand by watching you make yourself sick on purpose. Elizabeth, I can't! I won't!"

"Lizard, Elizabeth, what your mom means is..." Dad tried to smooth things over as usual, but I wasn't having it.

"Dad, don't. Mom has been pretty clear with what she means. You both have been working against me, to rid me of this gift I was given. To keep me home. I understand it would be easier for everyone if I were just normal. If I didn't disappear for days or weeks at a time. If I were able to go to school, get a normal job, have normal relationships. At one point, I wished I was different too, but I have learned to accept that this is how life is for me. I wish you would accept this too. This is who I am, and it's never going to change!"

After my last attempt for them to hear me out, I left the room. Mom started to say something else, but I couldn't argue about this anymore. At this point, we were just going to argue in circles. This all comes down to one simple fact, they still haven't accepted this part of me after all this time, and are still trying to change me. It hurts. I know they love me, but it sometimes feels conditional. Like it is easier to love me, when I fit into their lives, when I'm not going anywhere.

I'm writing this crying. I feel like my world is spinning out of control. I should mention that my one day/evening at the amusement park equalled two weeks here at home. I don't understand why. I thought with the drugs, I could have shorter trips more often, and not be gone for so long.

I'm losing time, I'm losing my best friend, I'm afraid my parents are going to do something drastic, and I'm not even sure I really know the guy I am risking all this for.

EVERYTHING SUCKS

I'm laying in bed right now, no, correct that, I'm practically shackled to my bed. I'm connected to an IV drip, and a couple of machines that apparently Dad can monitor when not in the room, so I have been warned not to tamper with it.

What's the point anyway, I just don't care about anything anymore.

Am I being dramatic? Yup, probably, but I think anyone in my position would eventually find themselves where I am now. All I want is a life, but because the life I live is different than everyone else, I am constantly fighting for it. Fighting against everyone, who wants me to have a life, but on their terms. After Lotus spilled all my secrets, the stupid intervention, and now my fight with Gabe, I just feel done.

My fight with Gabe. That was fun. I might as well relive that right now, because it's not like I could feel any lower.

After my intervention, I needed to see Gabe, the one person who I thought would be sympathetic. I needed to vent. I needed a hug.

I stayed up the entire night after my fight with my parents. Because I was already exhausted and depleted from my last trip, I was able to leave the following morning. This was a first for me. I have never travelled days apart like that. I was so relieved, I needed to get out of my house.

I found myself at a train station. If that wasn't perfect symbolism, then I don't know what is.

This place was a beautiful, old brick building. It looked like it could have been hundreds of years old, but it also could have been brand new, depending on this Earth's development. Above me, the roof was a dome made of glass and intricate ironworking.

I was standing on a platform, one of many, that separated many tracks. It was a gloomy, rainy day. It felt like it could have been mid-afternoon, but without a clock anywhere nearby, I didn't know for sure. A train station without clocks seemed a little weird to me. You would think the time would be plastered everywhere in a place that runs on schedules. Maybe here, things worked differently.

The station wasn't busy. I would say it was close to being empty. Besides myself, I saw maybe three other people, standing on other distant platforms. I knew I would see a fourth soon, and sure enough, Gabe entered the platform, heading toward me.

I hadn't noticed, but I was physically sobbing when I arrived. Gabe did notice, so when he reached me, he said nothing but took me in his arms. It was exactly what I needed. I felt safe, protected, understood, loved. It was too easy to lose myself in his arms, to forget everything.

But I didn't want to forget. Not this time.

"Don't. Don't do that" I pulled out of his arms and pushed him away.

"Do what? Why, what's wrong?"

"Don't be so perfect, so that I lose myself again." I started.

"Lose yourself? Elizabeth, I don't know what you mean. Please, tell me what's going on?"

"Yes, what *is* going on?" I asked back. "I need answers, and I want them now!"

"Ok, of course. Let's go find a place where we can talk."

"We can talk right here, right now." I motioned to a bench for us to sit on. "This is as far as I am going. No distractions, just talking."

"Sure, that's fine, whatever you want." He was being so agreeable and for some reason, it was pissing me off. "I am so surprised to see you again so soon."

"Well, life at home just completely fell apart. Lotus told my parents everything, my parents are fighting with me about it, so I successfully ran away, only to remember that I have a boyfriend, who I know nothing about, because every time I want to ask you any questions related to you, I always somehow forget, or get distracted, but not in a natural way. It feels like I am being manipulated, and it feels like you might be involved." I'm pretty sure I said this all very fast, with one breath.

"You think I am manipulating you?" He looked hurt.

I further explained what I meant, and how I have been trying to learn just the basic information about him without any success. I then went full crazy and told him my theory about how I suspect he can control my travelling, and determine where we go, to manipulate my mood, and keep me distracted. While I spoke, Gabe listened, but his expression switched from compassion, to confusion, and finally showed no expression at all.

"Is this what you really think of me?" Gabe finally asked, after we sat in silence for a few minutes.

"I just need answers. We can't move forward in our relationship until I get some."

"And I don't have a say in this?" He asked hesitantly.

"A say in what? I'm not asking for anything crazy. What are you hiding?"

"I'm not hiding anything, it's just that my answers are complicated, and I feel like if I tried to explain them, it would just sound too outrageous and I would lose you."

"So instead, I'm just supposed to do what? Follow you blindly, without knowing who you actually are, or what you can actually do? Just be a good girl, know my place, and do whatever you think is best for us?"

"When have I *ever* talked down to you or treated you like you weren't my equal!" Gabe was angry. I had never seen him remotely mad, and it was a bit alarming, but I wasn't going to let it stop me from getting what I needed. He continued, "I am not saying I don't want to tell you everything you want to know. I'm just saying that I have been waiting for the right time."

"Can't you see how sketchy that sounds? Do you not have the concept of red flags where you are from?" I might have sounded a bit too bitchy here, but I had already gone full crazy, so why not just show him all the undesirable sides of me.

"I don't care how it sounds, that is the truth."

"So what is the plan Gabe, be this perfect version of you, be the perfect boyfriend, make me fall hopelessly in love with you, become dependent on you, and only then will you tell me all your secrets? Get me attached so that whatever it is you tell me, it will be too hard for me to leave?"

"Why do you think everyone is conspiring against you? Elizabeth, I have shown you, I am showing you who I really am. This is me. I'm not trying to deceive you." He pleaded.

"Then please, help me feel a little less crazy and clear things up for me!"

He sat there for a few moments, angry and wounded, not saying anything. Looking back, I don't blame him. I didn't even try to understand where he was coming from. I offered no compromise. I decided I should get what I wanted, no matter the cost to him. I guess this has become a common recurrence in my life. I'm surprised he gave me any answers at all.

"I am not manipulating you." He started, his voice low and sad. "I can't control where you travel to. I can only feel you and hope to find you. I don't know why you forget your questions when you are around me. Nor have I ever purposely tried to distract you from remembering."

"But when I have asked in the past, you have been vague with your answers, or switched topics." I reminded him,

"Yes, when we first met, that is true. I wasn't ready to tell you then." He admitted.

"And you're not ready to tell me now"

"I have been waiting ..."

"Waiting for the right time, yeah you said." I rudely interrupted. "Gabe, I'm not asking you to solve some complicated mystery to the meaning of life! I just want to know who you are, who am I spending all this time with? Who have I gotten to know more intimately in some ways than I have with anyone else? Why is it so hard for you to tell me?"

"Dammit Elizabeth, because I don't know!" He wasn't yelling but his voice was raised louder than was comfortable. "I don't know who I am, or where I am from!"

"What? How is that possible?" I was beyond confused."Where do you go when your trip is over? You're not making any sense." His answer was not good enough for me, so I kept pushing, even though his emotional response warned me that I shouldn't.

"We both can travel to parallel universes. Our clothes magically change when we arrive, pockets filled with money, if we need it, we don't get hungry, thirsty, or tired, and yet, this sounds impossible to you? I just don't know, and if that isn't a good enough answer for you..." He trailed off.

He reached his breaking point. He stood up, faced me, and took a breath as if he were going to finish his thought, but instead, he shook his head and walked away.

I assumed he just needed time and would be back, but he never came back. He left, and I sat there alone for hours, waiting to go home.

I spent the first hour crying. I was so overwhelmed with emotions, so that was all I could do. When my body was cried out, my mind punished me further by reliving everything that had just happened, over and over again. Every moment was analysed down to every word that was spoken, how it was said, and the emotions that were felt and shown.

It soon became clear to me that despite how desperate I was feeling, I could have handled this better. Whether I deserve answers or not, I should have waited to bring this up to Gabe when I wasn't so emotionally driven. If I would have just let him comfort me, he would have let me vent about what happened at home, and I might have been in a better head space to deal with everything.

Now everything just feels hopeless. Gabe left, and I don't blame him. I was awful. Things are not good with my parents, and at this point, I don't know if I have it in me to forgive Lotus, and even if I did, I'm not sure if she would hear it.

When I got home from the train station, I must have fallen asleep immediately. When I finally woke up, Dad had already finished his examination. I was connected to a few machines, and my arm was plugged into an IV drip. My half day at the train station equalled three weeks at home. Dad wants me in bed for a week or two, because leaving twice so close together has left me very weak. I'm allowed to get up to use the washroom, and that is it. This is the weakest I have ever felt, so I wasn't going to fight him.

It's not like there was any point in fighting anything anymore. At this point, I don't want to travel. If I travel, I'm afraid of what will happen when I see Gabe, but in truth, I am more afraid that I won't see him at all.

So my parents and Lotus win. I'll just let them pump me full of whatever drugs they want, and just spend the rest of my life locked up and miserable.

EVERYTHING
SUCKS A BIT LESS

I t has been two months since my fight with Gabe. I haven't travelled since the train station.

A part of me is relieved that I haven't gone anywhere. In fact, I have been actively trying to stay home. But a growing part of me desperately wants to see him and make things right. I'm just afraid it might be too late.

My health scare after my last trip has brought me and my parents closer together. On my end, not wanting to travel has meant getting adequate sleep, taking all medication, and trying to eat properly. My parents may have interpreted this as me finally listening to them and their concerns. I didn't correct them, and just let them think what they wanted. After a month, when my parents saw that I was making a real effort towards my health, I think maybe they decided to put a bit of effort into trying to understand my life more. Well, that part of my life they have been trying hard to get rid of.

Despite my health improving from my last trip, I find I get tired very easily and have lost a bit of strength.

It has been frustrating feeling like this, especially since I have been working so hard toward maintaining healthy habits. Mom made a comment that she is afraid that I have fallen into a deep depression. In truth, I have. I was basically going from my bed, to the couch, back to my bed. I had no appetite, and showering wasn't happening as often as it should. I had gotten to a point where I just didn't feel like doing anything, and just didn't feel anything anymore. My depression worried my parents so much that, despite how she felt about it all, Mom said she was open to talking about my recent trips. She suspected something had to have happened to bring me down so low, and suggested that talking about it might help bring me out of this depressed state. She promised to keep an open mind when I felt like talking. It was nice that she was offering to push her feelings aside, for the sake of my mental health.

In time, I took Mom up on her offer. Even though she promised to be open about everything, she admitted that it was still going to be difficult to talk about this, but she wanted to be here for me and would try her best. We decided that when she had enough, we would take breaks, and we would both sit and talk again when we were ready.

For her to understand how I got to where I am now, I started from the beginning. She knew how I met Gabe. I had mentioned him when I told her and Dad about my narrow escape from that village that was being executed. I explained how our relationship progressed, and my recent struggles with it.

Finally, we got to my last trip. I explained how my fight with Gabe destroyed me. It's not the fact that we fought. I think it's healthy for people in a relationship to be able to argue. It's the possibility that I may never see him again. I'm so afraid that I screwed things up so badly that I won't get the chance to try to fix it, or at least apologize, and say a proper goodbye. He looked so hurt and defeated when he walked away. Knowing that I did that to him has been hard to live with.

It was so good to talk to Mom about all this again, and I like to think she felt the same way. Not only did she listen, but took an active part in the discussions. She mirrored my emotions, showing excitement when I told her about my first kiss, and shared in my heartbreak when I recently made the realization that I think I was in love with Gabe, which makes everything hurt so much more.

I didn't talk boys with Dad, but I did allow him to discuss my health, without my usual dismissal, taking it seriously for once, which brought us a bit closer together. We watched a few baseball games together and streamed some concerts. It wasn't the same as it was before when we could go to such events together in person, but it was nice just to hang out with Dad again.

A few nights ago my parents and I decided that we were all ready to discuss everything that had recently happened. We needed to get everything out in the open, and not one topic would be off-limits. Ground rules were made. Everyone would get a turn to speak and be heard, without interruption. The goal was to try to understand each other's point of view, why they did what they did, try to come to an understanding, and hopefully move on with a clean slate. Lotus showed up at our house before our meeting began. My parents invited her, deciding she needed to be a part of this, and I am so thankful they did.

The evening started out awkward and polite. I knew this was not going to get us anywhere, so I dove right into the discussion, bringing up the medication. I told them how I felt about it, (which I have written about here so many times, I don't think I need to again), and everyone agreed that they shouldn't have lied about it. In return, my parents justified why they chose to do what they did, and in the end, I agreed that I have not been easy to deal with, especially when it comes to my well-being, so I understood why they chose to do what they did.

Acknowledging that I put my health on the line for a guy was hard to do, but let's be honest, that is what I did, and I owned up to it. I made them understand that I wasn't trying to make myself sick, but I was careless and ignored potential consequences to my health by trying to make myself leave for a trip, instead of letting it happen naturally. They admitted they understand what it is like to have that first love, and that it makes you do stupid things. They also brought forward their concerns about Gabe possibly enabling this behaviour, but I assured them that he was on their side and that I might not have been truthful with him about how my recent travels have been affecting me. (Must remember to add that to my long apology list, if I ever get to see him again.)

Lotus came to our meeting prepared with a folder of paperwork. All her reasons for her betrayal were listed and then written out in long form. She wrote out arguments and counterarguments. She was prepared for me to be angry, and to fight back, and wanted to be able to argue with facts, instead of emotions. (She is going to be an amazing lawyer, like my mom). She was prepared to prove to me how she was being a good friend, by going behind my back, despite what I thought. Unfortunately, all her effort was wasted, because before she had a chance to speak, I not only forgave her but thanked her.

If it wasn't for Lotus emailing my parents, this night would not have been possible, and I expressed this to her. I know I was being stubborn about everything because my parents weren't budging about the truth on their end. She not only saved all our relationships, but she also further prevented my health from declining more than it already had. After a crap load of self-reflection, I was able to admit that I was not being a good friend by making her keep the kind of secrets that I had asked her to keep.

Long story short, we all worked through everything. Apologies were made, forgiveness was given, my parents and I are finally back on good terms, and I have my best friend back.

Lotus was allowed to stay for a few nights. We had a lot to talk about since it has been four months since we last spoke.

She ended things with 'Mall Guy' (I swear, she keeps telling me his name, but I can never remember it) and is currently single. She has been busy updating her wardrobe for college and is looking forward to starting classes. She showed me pictures from her prom, and she looked amazing, as usual. (She wore a silver sparkly dress, and looked like she walked off a runway during Paris fashion week.) I recognized some faces in the photos from when I went to school, which feels like a lifetime ago. It was bittersweet. I'm so happy for everyone, but at the same time, the photos reminded me of the life I never got to have.

I updated Lotus on my Gabe drama. She agreed that I handled it all wrong, but still thinks there is hope that he will talk to me again. I hope she is right. For now, I am not ready to find out.

PROMISES

Despite my, and my parents' efforts to keep me home for a while, I travelled.

I came home two days ago. After my post-vacation medical, and a hearty meal, (Mom made her lasagna! So good!) I crashed for almost a day and a half. When Dad was examining me, he told me I was gone for seventeen days. It was only two days for me.

Let's get right into it.

I arrived in what looked like an old European city, at least this is how it would look on our earth. This could have been a completely normal city here, but this place undoubtedly had history. The roads were cobblestone, and most buildings were made of brick and stone, while others were grand and an architectural dream, which compared to a lot of our Earth's churches, government buildings, and buildings or castles owned by royalty or nobility. With modern vehicles filling the streets, coupled with technology all around, this proved to me that this Earth's timeline could be very close to ours. I would have almost thought I was in any European city back home, except the cars just looked a bit different, everything just looked a bit off. I honestly don't know if I could describe it properly.

When I arrived, I immediately started walking to take in as much scenery as possible. This place was not only beautiful, it just felt magical. When I was young, my parents took me to Paris for a week, so I found myself referring back to those memories. I don't really remember too much about that vacation, because I was only seven, but I remember how I felt while there, and the feelings were very similar here at this place.

Even though there were cars everywhere, pedestrians were made a priority. There were a lot of roads dedicated to only foot traffic and bicycles. On busy main streets, there were pedestrian bridges that allowed you to cross safely over the traffic. It made walking easy, safe, and so enjoyable.

The smells! Holy crap this place smelled so good. I swear, there was a bakery on every corner pumping out that fresh bread and pastry smell.

Everyone spoke a language I didn't know. I can tell you that it wasn't English or French. There is a chance it could have been a language that we don't have on our Earth, but really, what do I know? I'm not a language expert. On a few occasions, I thought it would be cool to learn a new language. I have tried French, Spanish, and German. I can say a few swear words in each of these languages but that is all I could retain.

I think Gabe was always in the back of my mind while I walked around. I was still divided as to whether I wanted to see him or not. If I did see him, I knew I absolutely needed to apologize to him. I pushed him too far and didn't think about his feelings. I made peace with the fact that an apology doesn't mean we will get back together, and he might not forgive me. I just needed him to know that I know I was in the wrong, and how truly sorry I am for how I treated him. He didn't deserve it.

On the other hand, if I didn't see him that was also telling. He knows when I travel, so he knew I was there. If he didn't show up, it meant that he wasn't interested in an apology, or maybe didn't think I was capable of one. Whatever his reason, he was finished with me. I had to be prepared for both scenarios.

I probably walked for a good three hours straight, admiring the scenery, being a typical tourist. I finally stopped when I found a cafe that was situated alongside a river that ran through the city. It was so picturesque, so I decided to sit at one of their outdoor bistro tables and take in the view while I had something to eat. Before I sat down I checked to see if I had any money. I did. I should also mention what I was wearing. I had on a long flowy, light grey skirt, with a white tank top, and white strappy sandals. On my back was a small black backpack-type purse, which is where I found some spending money, sunglasses, and lip balm. Definite essentials.

To my relief, the servers spoke English. I was feeling bold, so I ordered the charcuterie board for one and a glass of red wine. They didn't ask for any identification, so either I looked older than my age, or the drinking age was lower here. I felt so fancy. I nibbled on my cheese, crackers, fruits and pieces of bread while I watched small boats float lazily down the river.

"Would it be ok if I joined you?" It was Gabe! He was standing behind the empty chair across the table from me, with a cautious smile.

"Yes, yes of course," I replied.

For a brief second, his smile reached his eyes, but when he sat down, caution was all that remained.

A server came by our table immediately after Gabe sat down to take his order. He asked for a cappuccino and some fancy pastry.

"I wasn't sure if I would see you here...or again," I blurted out. I couldn't just say "hi" first?

"Honestly, I wasn't sure either, but curiosity got the better of me." He explained.

"What are you curious about, exactly?" My heart was going crazy at this point. It felt like it was preparing me for so many answers.

"This is the first time I felt you travelled in over three months. Since, well, since the last time I saw you. I was starting to think that maybe I lost the ability to feel you." He was very careful with his words. Guarded.

"Oh...right, well, since the train station, I have been home. This is my first trip since then." I honestly didn't know how to react. Was he worried about losing his ability to track me, or was he worried about me?

"Does that mean you have stopped trying to control your travelling? Or has it just not happened?"

He was making small talk, and it was killing me. Small talk in general makes me cringe, especially with strangers. I would rather stand awkwardly in silence than talk about the weather. This small talk was so much worse because it was avoiding, well, more like postponing the hard talk we needed to have. If I have learned anything this year, it is that difficult conversations need to be had at some point, and the sooner the better.

"Gabe, I'm so sorry. I was awful to you..."I started.

"Elizabeth, it's ok. You were having a bad day, I -" He interrupted.

"No!" I interrupted him. "It's not ok. Nothing about how I treated you is ok. True, I felt like my world was falling apart. I felt like no one understood or even tried to understand what I was going through, but when I vented to you and demanded answers from you, I was treating you the same way I was being treated. I pushed when I should have listened. I was so selfish, putting my feelings above yours." I needed to get it all out. I probably said a lot more, but this was the gist of it.

After I finished speaking we sat there for a few minutes in silence. I watched him take a sip of his drink, and rip pieces off his pastry. I would have paid top dollar to get inside his head, to find out exactly what he was thinking. Honestly, the silence was killing me, and I so desperately wanted to break it, but this wasn't about me, so I would give him all the time he needed.

"Thank you." He finally said.

I waited for him to say more because it felt like there was more, but he went back to picking at his pastry. He looked like he was contemplating whether he should have come or not, at least that is how I was interpreting it. This time I did break the silence.

"Gabe, I think you are still upset with me," I observed.

"I mean, yeah, I appreciate the apology, and that you realize how you treated me was wrong, but some things were said that hurt, still hurt, and I am not sure how to move on from that."

"I know," I said sadly. "And I realize that after we talk here today, you may choose to not continue with our relationship or friendship. I get it, and I will respect your decision." I was fighting back a tear or two here.

"You thought I was manipulating you." He jumped right in.

"I know, I'm sorry"

"Do you still feel that way now?" he asked.

"No, not at all," I answered.

"And why not?"

"Honestly, during our fight, when I saw how upset that accusation made you, I knew I had it all wrong," I admitted.

"I'm not even that upset that you thought I was manipulating, and controlling you. I mean, I am, but I am more upset with how you brought it up. I understand that you have been trying to ask me questions and for some reason, you get distracted, but to assume that it was my doing. You could have come to me and expressed your frustration with what was happening. We could have talked things through and tried to figure it out together. Instead, you accused me of being this horrible person. And perhaps if you talked to me about this, I could have explained why answering personal questions is hard, and why I needed time. I just assumed you were giving me that time because you hadn't brought it up. We both made assumptions because we weren't open with each other."

This has been a common theme in all my relationships lately, and I feel just awful that Gabe was included.

"You're right," I confirmed

"You agree with me?" I think maybe he was expecting some pushback from me.

"Of course I do. This may be a poor excuse, but I think the reason I was so quick to blame you was that all my relationships had become so strained. With so much lying and deception going on for so long, I think it was just easier to think you weren't being honest with me too. I know how screwed up that is…"

"You didn't even give me a chance, or the benefit of the doubt." Gabe chimed in.

"No, I didn't. I have zero clue how any of this is possible. How am I able to transport to other places? Why have I only met one other person who can? Why am I taken to the specific places I have visited? Why does it sometimes feel manipulated? I have so many questions, and there are so many unknowns, but I do know now that it wasn't fair to put some of the blame on you, to make it make sense to me. I absolutely should have brought all this up with you, as you said. We could have tried to figure out some of this together."

We sat in silence again, but I welcomed it. It gave both of us a chance to properly absorb everything that was said, and to allow ourselves to really think about what we wanted to say next. I know there was more I could say, but I think it would just come across as begging for forgiveness. Maybe it all came across like that. Either way, I couldn't help myself and spoke again.

"Gabe, if I could take it all back, and do it all over again, I would in a heartbeat. Knowing I hurt you has been one of the most painful things I have dealt with lately. I can't say that I have changed since the last time I saw you, because I don't believe someone can change who they are that quickly, but I need you to know that I have, and still am making changes to do better." I promised myself that I was done talking at this point, it was his turn to guide the conversation.

"Tell me about the changes you are making."

"It's somewhat of a long story, I would need to backtrack through the last few months," I warned him.

"I have time if you do. But we should probably order something else before we lose this table." He suggested.

So that is what we did. We both decided on a tray of desserts to share, we each got a fresh cappuccino and I filled him in on everything that had happened at home.

I left nothing out. I told him about how I fell into a deep depression, how my mom helped me out of it, the intervention, how I made up with Lotus, and how I am working to improve my health. I told him about my self-reflection and how I realized how truly selfish I have been. He let me speak without any interruptions, except for a few clarifying questions here and there. I also admitted, for the sake of being open and honest with him, how I tried not to travel, and my reasons why. He told me he understood. We both needed some time.

When I was finished explaining what I had been up to, I asked him what he had been doing. He admitted that after about a month when he hadn't felt me travel, he started going on random trips to see if he could find me. Not necessarily to talk to me, but to see if our link had been severed. He was worried that when he walked away from me and left me at the train station, our bond was forever lost. Besides that, he didn't have much to tell me. I thought it was a bad sign that he didn't go into detail about the places he visited as he would always do, but maybe we just weren't there yet. When he was finished talking, I decided to let him make the next move, so I could maybe get a tiny grasp of what he was thinking or feeling. At this point, I was still prepared for him to say goodbye.

Gabe took the last sip of his drink and stood up. My heart started sinking. It was going to be truly difficult to say goodbye to him, but I had to respect his decision. He pushed in his chair and stood there for a second with his hands resting on the back of the chair, looking around.

"Do you want to walk around? Do some exploring?" He finally asked.

I was not expecting him to ask that. I nodded my head yes because I was speechless.

The day was coming to an end, and the street lights had started to turn on. Even though it was becoming dark, the city life gave no signs to show that it was slowing down.

While we walked, he admitted that he had walked for a few hours alone before trying to find me. He wanted to show me some of his favourite buildings and areas he had found, and then I returned the favour by showing him my favourite places. A lot of our favourite spots overlapped, while the others we showed each other were new to both of us. We kept the conversation light and only spoke about our observations on our walk, just as we did in the beginning when we were first getting to know each other.

We walked around for most of the night. We were both surprised by the amount of activity there was. The city just didn't sleep. Just before dawn, we came across a park that overlooked another river that ran through the city. Or maybe it was the same one? I don't know. By Gabe's calculations, the sun should rise above the water, so we found the perfect spot in the park to watch.

As we sat, I expected to sit in silence, and at first, we did. It didn't feel awkward, but completely comfortable to just be with him. A part of me was worried that the last eightish hours or so of pleasantry was just a prolonged goodbye, which would allow us to leave on friendly terms. If we were ever to bump into each other again, it would hopefully not be too awkward.

"I don't want to walk away from you..." Gabe spoke

low and softly.

"But?" I knew there was a but.

"But, you hurt me, and I'm worried about it happening again." he finished, quickly.

"I get that. I completely understand. Honestly, I can sit here and promise you that I would never ever hurt you again, but I don't think that is a promise anyone can guarantee."

"No, it's not." He said, in quiet contemplation. He continued, "You didn't ask the question."

"What question?" I was genuinely confused.

"When we last spoke, I admitted that I didn't know who I was, or where I was from. This bothered you. I just figured you would have brought this up at some point tonight. Don't you still want to know?"

"Yes, of course, but I only want to know when you are ready to tell me, and I didn't think it was appropriate to even bring it up tonight."

"No, it wasn't. I'm still not ready to explain everything, how do you feel about that?" He asked

"It doesn't upset me. Not anymore. I can wait. I can wait for as long as you need. Saying that, if we do continue to see each other, I need to slow us down until that time comes."

"Slow us down, how?" It was his turn to be confused.

"Ok, this is embarrassing, so I'm just going to say it. After my birthday, and before the train station, I was ready to give you all of me, if you get what I am saying. I just want to know who I am giving myself fully to."

"I wouldn't expect anything less from you." He reassured me.

"So what now?" I asked.

"Now, we make a promise to each other that from now on, we will be open and willing to talk to each other about anything and everything. It doesn't matter how difficult, awkward, silly, or weird the topic is. And after we make this promise to each other, I'm hoping to take your hand, and hold it while we watch the sunrise, and then, if we are lucky, we will have the day together."

And that is what happened. We were lucky to have most of the day together. We walked around and just hung out. It felt so good to be with him again. We both kept expressing how much we loved this place, and how we wished we could come back. We knew Gabe could come back. He has the ability to revisit places he has already been to. He suggested that when I know I am going to leave for my next trip, I try to focus on this place, picturing it in my mind, and try to will myself to come here. I told him I would try my best.

It was early evening when I knew it was time for me to go. It felt too soon for both of us. He kissed me softly, and like many times before, held me until I was gone.

UPDATE

A few days after I returned home from my European-esque vacation my parents sat me down for a talk. I knew what this would be about. They asked if my leaving was provoked or if I left naturally like I used to. I told them that the trip was a surprise to me, and assured them that I had kept my promise and had been taking all medications as well as still working on my healthy habits. I even offered to take blood tests to prove I had been taking my meds, but they told me they trusted me.

Mom and Dad told me they have made peace with the fact that they can no longer prevent my travelling. This last trip has proven that, despite all of our best efforts to keep me home the last few months, travelling was inevitable. This was a huge step for all of us. My parents promised me that they would no longer work against me, trying to prevent me from travelling, as long as I keep up my end of the promise, and not *try* to leave again. They would support me by helping to rehabilitate my body when I come home and to be there for any emotional support that I may need. My last trip left me extremely weak again. My recovery is taking longer every time I come back home. Besides all that, we would enjoy the time we have together as a family when I am home and worry about my travelling when it happens.

Time. I don't understand why, but my absence from home has become longer with each trip. I'm assuming this is the cause of my weakened state. Mom and Dad keep mentioning how time is precious, and they won't want to spend the time I have at home, fighting and arguing with me, which is why they have come to this peaceful disposition.

I filled Mom and Lotus in about Gabe. Obviously, I went into greater detail with Lotus than I did with Mom. Dad has no interest in hearing about boys, but I know he gets second-hand information from Mom, which I think is better that way. I knew Lotus would be happy for me, but I was surprised to see Mom was as well. She actually admitted to me that she was happy that I have Gabe, explaining it made the thought of me being out there, wherever I go, a little easier, knowing I am not alone and protected.

Mom is still worried that one day I won't want to come home, and the rekindling of my relationship with Gabe has further sparked that fear. She asked me if I was still writing down everything in my journal, and I assured her that I have been keeping an up-to-date account with as much detail as I can, of everything that has happened.

So now, it's a waiting game. Do I desperately want to see Gabe? Hell yes! But we both agreed that I need to let it happen naturally. He wasn't happy when I admitted to him how sick I made myself, trying to see him more often. Gabe said we basically have a long-distance relationship, and he isn't wrong. Unfortunately, the distance is so vast that it can't be measured, and we can't call or text in between meetings. He isn't worried, and neither am I. A lot of people make the long-distance thing work.

I'LL BE HOME FOR CHRISTMAS

Christmas is in two days, and I almost missed it. I have never missed a major holiday, (missing my birthday or Lotus's doesn't count), so I am relieved I made it home in time. My parents were overcome with joy when I came home too.

Time to backtrack a bit.

I left only three weeks after my last trip. I was surprised that I had left so early, I honestly wasn't expecting to leave until sometime after the new year. I was away for three days, which I believe was my longest trip yet, but unfortunately, that translated to my longest absence from home, four weeks.

When I felt the nausea, I said goodbye to my parents and lay down in my bed waiting to leave. I remembered what Gabe had suggested, so I concentrated on thinking only of the last city I had visited and tried to imagine myself going there.

It didn't work.

I found myself in an open field, standing in wildflowers, that stretched out as far as my eyes could see. Surrounding me were picture-perfect snow-capped mountains. It was very "Sound of Music" or at least, I assume so. I never actually watched that movie, but I have seen that blonde lady twirling around so many times in reference to it.

After about a minute of gawking at the mountains, probably mouth opened, but no drool, I have some class, I heard footsteps behind me. I turned around and saw Gabe walking toward me, wearing that smile that I had missed so much. When he reached me, he swiftly took me into his arms and kissed me.

"Is everything ok? I didn't think I would see you so soon." He was worried that I manipulated my travelling again.

I assured him I didn't and that I had come to this place naturally. He noticed my displeasure with where we were. I explained that even though this place was incredible and seemingly private, I was hoping to go back to the last place we visited. I explained that I tried to send myself there, obviously unsuccessfully.

"Do you trust me?" Gabe suddenly asked.

"What, why?" I had no idea what he was getting at.

"Do you trust me to try something?" He somewhat clarified.

"What do I have to do?" I seriously have always hated these kinds of questions.

"Just take my hand, don't let go, close your eyes and stand still. And maybe don't open your eyes until I tell you to." He explained.

"What the hell." I gave in to him, took his hand, and did as he directed.

I couldn't tell you what happened. No, that's not true, I can tell you what happened, and I will, but I don't know how it happened. With my eyes closed, I could feel this energy envelop us. It sort of felt like a gentle vibration in the air and I could hear a dull sound of electricity. I should have felt scared, but Gabe's touch kept me calm. When all the weird sensations went away, Gabe whispered in my ear to open my eyes.

I hesitated, but then slowly opened my eyes. The sun was bright, so it took me a few seconds for my eyes to actually see anything. When my eyes finally adjusted, I was standing beside a familiar bistro table, belonging to a cafe situated on a river.

He had brought me back!

"Holy sh-, how the f-, what! How?" I never claimed to be articulate.

"After you left last time, it got me thinking. If you couldn't send yourself here, maybe there was a chance that I could bring you back with me." He looked as surprised as I was that it worked.

We spared no time. Our table was free, so we sat and had a nice lunch. We were almost too excited about what happened to eat, but the food was too good, so we managed. We talked about all the possible things we could do together, and places we could go. We both decided that trying to travel together again too soon might be too risky, and we would save it for another time. In the meantime, I filled him in on what I have been up to for the last three weeks, which was not much at all, and he told me about some of the trips he took during the time of our fight.

After lunch we decided to further explore the city, wanting to get to know every inch of our new favourite place. We decided to make it our mission to try every single bakery, restaurant and bistro this city had to offer.

We checked two bakeries off the list that afternoon.

When we walked, we walked hand in hand. We would steal little kisses from each other here and there, and hugs were given in abundance. It felt like it used to before our fight, and I think we were both relieved by it.

Something strange happened while we were walking around. We had been walking for what felt like five hours. The sun was starting to set and some street lights were turning on, and I felt tired.

I have never gotten tired before. I don't feel anything like that when I travel, and neither does Gabe. I started to kind of freak out internally a little, but Gabe was observant and noticed the shift in my mood. I explained to him how I was feeling. He thought it was strange too, but didn't feel like I had to worry too much. He suggested that maybe my body is finally able to acclimatize to travelling. I pointed out that he had been doing this a lot longer than me without any acclimatization when suddenly he yawned.

This was a WTF moment for sure.

"You yawned!" I pointed at Gabe and stated the obvious.

"I did," Gabe replied, confused.

"Something must have happened when you brought me here. Like, maybe something activated when you chose to try to travel with me. It sort of makes sense, but yet none of this makes sense." This was me making sense out of nothing.

"That is all I can think of that we did differently. I think we definitely triggered something. I feel a bit tired, but also suddenly full from eating all that bread." Gabe said with instant regret.

As soon as he said that, I felt that too. I was tired

and full, and my legs started to ache from all the walking. Gabe's legs felt the same.

"What are we going to do about tonight? We will have to find someplace to stay." I was worried. We never had to worry about sleep before.

"I know a place where we can go, but first I have to tell you something."

"Okay..."I answered worriedly. Whenever someone has to tell you something or has to talk with you, chances are, it's not going to be something good.

"Elizabeth, it's not bad, I promise" He chuckled, as he led me to a bench, so we could rest our tired legs. "I have been waiting for the right time to tell you this today." He continued.

"Okay...."

He gave me a side glance, which told me I was being silly and then started to explain himself.

"I don't want you to think too much into this, but I have an apartment here. Before you say anything, I got it after you left the last time we were here. We both fell in love with this place, and I was hopeful that you would be able to return here one day with me. And even if you couldn't, I decided to make this place my home. I would travel to wherever you end up, and then when you leave, I would return here."

"Is it far from here?" I asked

"No, maybe a ten to fifteen-minute walk, but we don't have to go there. I mean, we can go hang out and rest, and then I can get you a hotel room if you aren't comfortable at my place. There is a hotel just down the street from me." He was acting nervous and it was adorable.

I said we could worry about one thing at a time

and asked him to lead us to his apartment. After a short walk, we arrived at his building. I had come across and admired this building before. The building was placed on a corner of two streets, with almost rounded architecture, and stood ten stories high. Each apartment had a little balcony constructed of black rod iron fencing, with intricate twisted designs. The building itself was surrounded by many shops and other apartment buildings, and many mature trees that lined the street.

Gabe had mentioned he was on the eighth floor. When we entered the building I was looking everywhere for an elevator. Gabe stood there laughing at me, and then finally told me there wasn't one and that we would have to take the stairs. This wouldn't have been an issue if we still didn't get tired. When we climbed up the first six flights of stairs, he mentioned that maybe he needed to rethink his apartment choice or at least work on his cardio.

After our long hike up, we finally reached the summit, his apartment. It was small but nice and bright. You entered the apartment into a small kitchen that opened to a living area. He had one bedroom, separate from the living area, and a small bathroom. He had two balconies which I thought was a nice touch. One was off the bedroom, and the other off the living room. They were only big enough for maybe a couple of chairs, or those small bistro table sets.

"I haven't really decorated or bought much stuff. I was waiting to see if you would be able to come back here, so you could help me." Gabe said.

"Yeah? I would love to help. Wait, where did you get the money to rent this?" I asked.

"I'm still trying to figure that out. When you left,

and I made the decision to stay here, I went to the bank to open a bank account with the pocket money I arrived with. I had a few hundred dollars. When I got to the bank, I opened my wallet and saw that I already had a bank card. The teller thought I was crazy to forget that I had an account. They told me the balance of my account and it was quite substantial. I don't get it, and I feel weird having so much money, not having worked for it." He explained.

"I wonder if that will change. Maybe now that we have triggered something or the fact that you are choosing to live here, maybe the money situation might change too, like run out and you might need to get a job. Then again, this place just feels so different. Magical even."

"That's a good point. I will keep an eye on it anyway. For now, I only want to buy what we need and live modestly, so I don't disrupt some sort of cosmic balance or whatever."

I assured him that I thought he had a good plan, as I sat on the couch to rest. He sat with me after pouring us some water and we started planning how to furnish and decorate his apartment. He had already bought a bed and a couch, so there wasn't much to talk about when it came to furniture, but I had a lot of ideas on how to spruce up the place. He liked a lot of my ideas, and I was relieved to find out we have similar tastes, but he did veto a few ideas. Like my idea of houseplants everywhere. Apparently, he can't keep a plant alive, despite his best efforts. I offered to take care of them, but we both agreed that might not be an option if I am not able to come back here again.

At one point during our conversation, I was having

a hard time keeping my eyes open, while Gabe was trying to hold back yawns. He insisted, as long as I was comfortable, that I take his bed, and he would sleep on the couch. After I accepted, we both agreed we were too tired to even walk to the hotel, so this was our best option. I fell asleep as soon as my head hit the pillow.

The morning was strange for us. Not just because this was our first sleepover, but because we were both hungry, had morning breath, and both needed some time in the washroom to clean up. I never had to worry about a change of clothes before, but with our bodies working normally now, fresh clean clothes were a must. Our task for the morning was to shop for some toiletries and a few outfits for him and myself.

After lunch, when we were freshly showered, dressed, and rested, we decided to venture out to do more exploring. We went to a few more bakeries and took note of others to try later. When fatigue got the better of us, we returned to his apartment much like the day before, talked for a while, (not talked for a while too), and I slept in his bed while he took the couch once again.

Two full days and nights with Gabe felt like such a gift. We both were afraid that I would leave at some point during the second night while we slept, so we said our goodbyes before retiring to our respective beds. To wake up in his apartment for a third day was a welcome surprise. We didn't waste a minute. We cleaned ourselves up, got dressed, and were out the door. I should also mention that the weather now affected us too. I had to buy some sunscreen when I noticed I started to burn yesterday.

We bought a few things for Gabe's apartment; dishes, an area rug, a lamp, and some towels. We checked a few more bakeries off our list to try and then headed back to Gabe's place. We decided to spend the last half of the day just hanging out. I have to mention how funny he is. He says the same about me. We laugh so much when we are together. It has become so effortless.

We were lying in his bed, talking and cuddling when I sensed Gabe's mood change slightly. It went from being light and playful to a bit serious.

"I'm ready to tell you everything," Gabe said suddenly.

"Ok, but only if you want to," I assured him.

"I do, I want to. I kind of need to. I just don't want to keep it to myself anymore."

"Ok" was all I could say, afraid I would say something stupid that would discourage him from continuing.

"At the train station, I admitted to you that I don't know who I am, or where I come from. Do you remember?"

Of course, I remembered. I remembered every word from that fight. I didn't say that to him though, instead, I just nodded yes.

"The truth is, when I am not travelling, I don't know where I go, or what I do. It's like this dark void in my memory. From a very young age I have learned that if I were to jump from place to place, if I kept choosing to travel, and not go home, I would retain who I am, and keep my memories. So that is what I have done, for most of my life." Gabe started.

"I have so many questions." I blurted out.
"I knew you would. Ask away, but know that there really isn't much more that I know or can tell you."

"Do you have parents? Any siblings?" I thought this

was a good place to start.

"I don't know. I mean, at some point I would have had to have had parents, but I just don't know." He sounded a bit sad.

"So, for me, when I return home, I have my life, and life at home continues like normal whether I am there or not, but when you are not travelling, you just return to nothing?" I clarified.

"Pretty much. I know the explanation sounds simple, yet impossible, but I don't know where I was born, who my parents are, why I can travel the way I do, or basically where I belong. I only know my name, and I am still unsure how I know that."

"Gabe, that is really sad."

"It is. I want to say that it got easier as I got older, but it didn't. Watching families everywhere I go just showed me what I was missing out on at every stage of my life." He explained.

"Is that why you were quick to defend my parents?"

"Yeah, I mean, I wasn't defending them, what they did was wrong, but I just wanted you to understand why they felt like they had to do what they did. In the end, I just wanted you and your family to be ok. I didn't want you to take them for granted. I would give anything to have normal fights and arguments with my parents."

"I wish I could take you home to meet mine. My mom would love you and I think my dad would eventually get over the idea of you, and maybe even warm up to you, at some point. Why do you think you can't travel to my home?"

"That is another thing I don't know. Since we developed this link, it disappears when you go home. I just stop feeling you. Why I can't go to your universe, but I can visit virtually any other makes no sense to me. I have tried so many times. I have also tried to find the version of you in other places when you are home and I have nothing to do. It's like you and I are the only unique people across all parallel worlds. We don't exist anywhere else that I can find."

"Is that why you are with me now? Because I am like you?"

"The truth is, I barely remember life before I met you, when we were kids, playing on that grassy field. All I know is that since then, when I felt you were different and when I thought you could be like me, I have spent my life trying to find you again, with no expectations other than friendship. I have always felt that you would become important to me, like you were sent to me. The fact that I completely fell in love with you was an unexpected, yet welcoming outcome."

Holy shit right? He had just told me he loved me. I can see why he wanted to wait to tell me his story. First, it was completely unbelievable. In order to believe it, you really have to get to know Gabe and his character. Second, it is hard to show your vulnerable side. He wanted to know who I was as a person and know he could trust me to handle this delicately and with compassion.

I was so focused on who he was to me, that I never stopped to think about who I was to him.

"I love you too" I replied, making sure I stated it clearly, so there would be no questioning what I just said or how I felt.

For a few moments, we just looked at each other. So many emotions passed between each other. It felt overwhelming and intense but in a good way. When the tension became too much, we found ourselves in each other's arms. We had made out many times by this point, but this felt different. It felt hungry, almost desperate. There was this sense of urgency like if we couldn't have each other right then and there, we would die. I told him that I needed him, all of him and that he may have all of me too.

I'm not going to go into detail about my first time for everyone to read. I'm not writing a smutty journal here. If Mom does publish my journal like she keeps threatening to do, I don't want my business printed all over the pages.

What I will say is that I had never felt such pure love and acceptance as I did during this time. The earth didn't stand still, nor were there any celebratory fireworks at the end. It was real, awkward, messy, painful, and yet so perfect.

Afterwards, when we were properly hydrated and regained a bit of our energy from a few snacks, we decided that it wouldn't be improper to share a bed at that point, and we fell asleep together for the night.

I'm not sure how long we had been asleep, but during the night I woke up feeling intense nausea. I quickly woke Gabe up, to say goodbye, so he wouldn't wake up to an empty bed, with no explanation. This was our hardest goodbye yet. As was our tradition, he kissed me and held me until I was gone.

NEW YEAR, NEW ME

Happy New Year!

Christmas came and went. It was amazing. I was still pretty weak from my last trip, but they propped me up in the living room, with my IV, so I wouldn't miss out on anything.

Lotus chose to come to stay with us that week. She has never missed a Christmas with her family, but she said she felt the need to celebrate it with me. She stayed with us from Christmas Eve and left on New Year's Day. My dad had the entire week off, staying available for emergencies, but luckily there weren't any. Together, we all watched our favourite holiday movies, decorated gingerbread, and played our favourite games. It was perfect. The only thing missing was Gabe.

I filled Mom and Lotus in on the details about my last trip. I told them how Gabe was able to bring me back to the city, and about his apartment. When Lotus and I were alone, I further filled her in on the rest of the details. She was beyond excited for me and kept saying I was a woman now. I do feel different. Not as different as I thought I would feel, but a bit different.

Mom got a bit emotional when I talked about

helping Gabe set up his apartment. She kept making comments about how it felt like I was setting up a new life away from home. I noticed Lotus hid her emotions when Mom was saying this too. I told them they were being a bit silly, as I always come back home. Mom reminded me, as she has been saying this for years, that there may come a day when I choose not to come home. Gabe has solidified that theory for her. She believes that one day, I will have to choose Gabe over home.

At that point, all three of us started bawling. Honestly, I think back now about it and it's pretty funny. The crying felt therapeutic for all of us. Dad walked into the room and quickly walked out. To his credit, he returned a few minutes later with tissues and a lot of chocolate.

Mom was right though. I have started to have that feeling, that one day I would have to choose, and it isn't fair. Why can't I have both, like so many other people have? Why can't Gabe come here, and choose to stay in my universe? He could have a family, and I wouldn't have to lose mine. On the other hand, it breaks my heart knowing that Gabe is alone right now. I am all he has.

Time has also led me to believe I will have to make this choice. The precious amount of time I get with Gabe has become an enormous absence here at home. For three days to equal a month here, how long will a week away become? Perhaps I am meant to eventually make this transition to another place, where time makes more sense. I would miss my family dearly, but what quality time do I get with them, or will get with them? I am writing this a few days after New Year, and I still have an IV attached to my arm. My recovery time is getting longer here, but when I am away, I feel healthy and strong.

I don't want to think about choosing right now. For now, I want to be a bit selfish and enjoy both lives I am currently living. I'm not ready to even think about saying goodbye to my parents or Lotus, yet I still need to see Gabe.

NEW POSSIBILITIES

I just returned home from seeing Gabe a few days ago. We just spent the most amazing four days together.

When I travelled, I arrived inside a ski resort, looking out to the snow, mountains, and all the skiers and snowboarders. It didn't take long for Gabe to find me. This place was incredible and grand, so we decided to stay and explore. We were in a bar or lounge-type area, where you can relax on comfortable chairs and couches and have a hot, or cold drink, after a day of outdoor recreation. I spotted a free couch by the fire, and we sat there, taking in the view. The fireplace was located in the middle of the room and was huge. The firepit itself was wide and open, so many people could gather around it from all sides. The fireplace was made of a grey stone that stretched to the ceiling. The Ceiling was decorated, (or maybe it was structural) with huge beams of wood. Wood was everywhere but in a tasteful sort of way. One wall consisted of just windows. As we sat, it started to snow. It was enchanting.

Gabe was being incredibly flirty as we sat and talked. Flirty and handsy, but I promise he was being respectful. Obviously, I flirted back. I was starting to worry that we would start catching someone's eye, but no one paid any attention to us. The flirting turned into a bit of frustration, at least on my end. After so much teasing, I was ready to find someplace private. He asked if I wanted to take a turn down the ski slopes. I told him I wanted to be back at his apartment, like ten minutes ago.

Gabe led me out of the public area to a secluded hallway. Much like the first time, he instructed me to take his hand, close my eyes and stay as still as I could. I felt that weird, low vibration of energy again, coupled with a dull sound of electricity. Seconds later, Gabe whispered in my ear to open my eyes, and we were in his apartment. Actually, he brought us right to his bedroom.

We spent the rest of the day, and half the night, entangled in romantic gestures.

The next day, over breakfast, we decided that while I was visiting, we would focus on experimentation. No, not that kind, this isn't some multiple shades of a colour-type scenario here.

Travel experimentation.

Gabe was able to find me and bring me back to his apartment so easily, so we wanted to see if there was any limit to this. We would pick a destination we have already been to, and see if we can make it there and back. We both thought it would be appropriate to start where we first met. He thought about the garden party, as he held my hand and we closed our eyes.

After the now familiar energy whoosh, I opened my eyes and found myself in a cherished memory. Not only did he bring us back to the castle grounds, but he managed to bring us back in time to that actual party. Either that, or this place is simply frozen in time, or has a bad case of Groundhog Day. You know, that movie your parents probably made you watch where the day is forever Groundhog Day. (It is one of Dad's favourite movies, so I have seen it a few times.) The castle was still under construction and had not made any progress. The tents, tables, food, band, and chairs, were all in the same places as I remembered them. I'm not going to describe it all again, but feel free to flip back to where I described it all before if you need a refresher. The only thing that changed was our outfits. It would have been awkward if we were wearing the same clothes as last time, as I was nine and Gabe was ten.

I was wearing a simple short-sleeved lilac dress. These dresses didn't hug you at the waist as most modern dresses would. The fabric hugged under my breasts and then flowed freely. Honestly, just watch Brigerton or any version of Pride and Prejudice. The women were dressed very similarly. My hair was somehow piled on top of my head, with selected curls coming down around my face. Gabe wore a dark blue tailcoat, with a white frilly shirt underneath, paired with tan-coloured trousers. He looked good, but he always does.

We arrived at the field where the kids were playing. They were playing the now familiar twirling game. Gabe took my hands and spun me around until it became too much for us. We were not kids anymore and agreed one turn was more than enough, unlike our many turns together the last time we were here.

It became obvious to us that this was a private event. There were many people here, but we assumed they were all invited. We thought it best to try to blend in without bringing attention to ourselves. We would avoid conversations, but try to look like we belonged. At least we looked the part.

We mostly hovered around the food and drinks. We had to be careful because alcohol now affected us and food made us full. We listened to the music and people-watched as we nibbled and drank. We decided to leave when the drinks started to make us feel a bit dizzy, and our feet hurt from standing. We didn't dare sit down, in case we sat in someone's seat.

We walked away from the party, found a tree to conceal our disappearing act, and went back to Gabe's.

Gabe assured me that bringing me back and forth is easy and requires no extra effort, but we remained cautious. On the third day, we quickly went to the "Sound of Music" field, spent ten minutes walking around, and then returned to his apartment. Again, Gabe felt fine, and there were no physical consequences.

This was a game-changer. We started making plans to go places that we had been before and wanted to show each other. We also would do some exploring of new places together. But for the rest of my trip, we decided to stick around the apartment. We weren't sure how long I was staying, so we took advantage of the privacy until I left.

I left for this trip at the end of January. I got home three days ago, to discover that it was the middle of March. To say I was surprised would be an understatement. Throw in 'shocked,' 'worried,' and a few 'WTFs.'

I let Mom smother me as much as she needed when I got home. The truth was, I needed it as much as she did. Dad got a few more hugs in than normal too.

It feels like I am in some sort of transition. My body thrives when I am away, but has been deteriorating here at home. I tried not to read too much into it, but it is becoming a hard fact to ignore. I think I'm just not ready to think about what it means. Not Yet.

I'M OK

I was hooked up to various machines and an IV for the last three weeks. Do you realize how much we take for granted being able to just get up and use the washroom so easily, and alone? For the first week, I had to take my IV and some other machine, I forgot what it was for, or what it did, but Dad insisted I needed it, to the washroom with me, with the help of Mom. I'm almost nineteen years old and I need my mom to help me use the washroom. In the last two weeks, I still had to take my IV everywhere, but I was able to do my business mostly alone. I say mostly because Mom would still hover outside of the washroom. She thought she was being stealthy, but I knew she was there. A year ago, I would have had words with her about respecting my boundaries and privacy, but now, I think it's sweet. She is worried about me, and I get that. I'm worried about myself too.

Recovery is still taking longer, but I am dealing with more physical problems now. Every time I leave, I come back with less muscle mass and less overall body weight. I am too skinny, and cold all the time. I'm trying to eat more, but I find my appetite comes and goes in waves. This is so frustrating, because I LOVE to eat, and

Mom and Dad have made sure to have all my favourite foods on hand recently. I have no energy either. Just walking from my bedroom to the living room makes me need a nap. My parents help me set up on the couch during the day and they bring me back to my room at night.

Lotus has been coming around a lot too. I keep asking "How am I getting so lucky with her frequent calls and visits?" She tells me she just misses me, and that she is finding University a bit lonely, and needs her best friend.

(Lotus, if you are going to lie to me, make sure next time you block me from your Instagram and Snapchat, so I can't see the fun you are actually having. Silly girl! I love you too.)

It is sweet that she would make up excuses to come see me. I'm not even mad that she isn't being straight with me about it like we had promised each other we would do. I know why she has been around.

Just like I know why Mom and Dad have all my favourite foods around, why my music is always playing in the background, and why Dad has been taking more time off recently.

They are afraid that the next time I leave, I am not coming back.

This is crap, complete nonsense, and I told them all that. I assured them that if and when I was ready to leave for good, I would tell them when it was time. Now is not that time.

I'M STILL HERE

Happy Birthday to me! More like Happy Birthday to me, two months ago. I was abroad and I missed my nineteenth birthday. I would have celebrated it while I was away if I knew I was going to be away for it, but there was no way I could have known that. I was away for only five days, leaving at the end of April, but when I returned home, it was mid-July. I lost so much time.

I have been back for almost two weeks now. I am feeling good today, and have a bit of energy, so I am taking advantage of that and will write about my recent trip. This is a difficult one for me to get through.

I arrived on a rocky, sandy beach. I was at a lake. The lake itself was surrounded by miles of dense evergreens and maples with private cottages tucked in them here and there. It looked like I was standing in a small public area, where anyone could come and enjoy the water, and where residents would launch their boats.

Like clockwork, Gabe found me shortly after I arrived. While looking for me, he said he saw an office close by with a sign that read "Cottages for Rent." We decided to see if there were any vacancies, and what was being offered.

There was one cottage left, available for four days. We took it immediately without even looking at it. Honestly, if it turned out to be a dump, Gabe would just take us back to his place. We both arrived with bank cards and money, so we paid for the rental in cash.

The cottage was a twenty-minute walk from the office, along a dirt road. The road was cut through the forest, making it feel like we were on a hike. We passed three cottages before we came to ours. Each cottage was private and secluded. You only really knew you were passing by one of the cottages by walking past the hidden driveways, or by a small pole marking the cottage with a number. We finally got to our cottage, number fifteen. We turned into the hidden driveway, and the trees finally opened up to reveal our home for the next few days. It looked small, but we didn't care. At least, we thought it was small. As we approached, it looked like a small one-level little house. When we entered, we realized that there was an entire bottom level, not seen from the road. The trees hid that we were on top of a hill, so there was a walk-out basement.

I'm getting ahead of myself. The first floor had a decent-sized kitchen, a small, cozy sitting area, a washroom, and the Master Bedroom. The master bedroom opened up to a deck that overlooked the property and the lake. The property itself wasn't big, but large enough to have a fire pit, and play some lawn games. The grass was perfectly green and manicured, which led to a sandy water's edge, and a private dock.

The basement had two more bedrooms, and a larger gathering area, complete with a wood fireplace. From there, you walk outside to a hot tub, and then you continue to the firepit, and eventually the water.

We honestly would have been happy with a one-room shack-type place, as long as there was a bed, and someplace nearby to get food. This was way beyond expectation.

When I arrived at the lake, I was wearing casual black shorts, and a white T-shirt, with light-tanned sandals. Underneath I wore a two-piece swimsuit, instead of a bra and underwear. Gabe was wearing a pair of dark blue board shorts, and a grey t-shirt, with black slip-on sandals. We were happy to have been wearing swimsuits but knew that one outfit would not last us four days. The cottage had a computer we could use, so we were able to order a few more pieces of clothing that would arrive the next day.

The rental office had given us a few numbers for food services who would deliver to the cottages. After we took care of the food and clothing situation, it was time to relax.

For the first few days of cottage life, we kept it light and fun. We had fun playing in the lake, relaxed in the hot tub, enjoyed a nice fire before bed, and enjoyed each other. It was during our last full day when the conversations became serious. We were in the hot tub when Gabe asked how everything was at home and what I had been up to since I last saw him. I had to tell him the truth. I told him how my body has become frail, and that it's not fully recovering anymore after I go home. I explained how my parents and Lotus have been acting like they are saying goodbye to me every time we talk.

"It's like your body is transitioning. Like it is preparing for you to stay here. You are perfectly healthy here, right now." Gabe observed.

I told him that is exactly what I said, and expressed these thoughts with my parents too.

We talked about how I am losing so much time, and how frustrating it is that when I am home, how it is spent feeling so sick and weak and being looked after, instead of spending quality time doing anything enjoyable.

"Then stay," Gabe suggested

"I think that might have to be an option at some point. I have to figure that out." I replied.

"What is there to figure out?"

"So much!" I exclaimed. "The logistics of everything, when I choose to stay. *If* I can choose to stay, where will -"

"You would stay with me." He said so matter-of-factly.

"Are you sure? I mean, I was always hoping you would want that, but I would never assume, or impose on you. I could get my own apart-" I started to ramble here.

"Elizabeth, I love you. I will never love anyone more than I love you. I will never want to be with anyone more than I want to be with you. I want to build a life with you, and ever since we figured out that I can choose to create a home anywhere, and bring you with me, I have been desperately wanting to ask you to stay with me."

"Why haven't you asked?" I couldn't help myself, I had to know.

"Well, first, our ages. Let's be honest, we are still so young. As much as my mind is made up about us, I don't want to rush you, and I don't want to rush taking you away from your family. And then there is your family. I have a feeling that once you make up your mind to stay, there will be no going back home. As much as I miss you when you are away, it would have been selfish to ask you to stay, knowing you have a full life away from me, so I couldn't ask. But now things are different."

"Yes, they are. I love my family and Lotus so much, but I am so tired of feeling so weak, and helpless. I know when I go back home I will be bedridden, and rely on machines to help my body function. I know I will have missed so much time and important dates. I feel like such a burden to everyone now. Their life shouldn't just be about looking after me anymore." At this point, I started to cry.

"You can stay now. If you feel like they have already said their goodbyes, then it may be time to let them go." Gabe suggested.

"They may have said their goodbyes, but I haven't. I'm not ready to leave them yet. You are right, we are young, I am way too young to have to make this kind of decision and it's just not fair."

"No, It's not fair." He agreed.

"GABE!" A wave of nausea suddenly hit me, and I started to panic. I reached out to him. "No, it's too soon! I can't go back yet!" Not only was I surprised that we didn't get more time together, but I wasn't ready to face what going home meant yet.

"Elizabeth, we are going to try something, and we have to try it right now." Gabe took my hands and tried his best to keep me calm with his soothing low voice.

"Ok, what do I do?"

"You are going to squeeze my hands, and in your mind, you are going to choose to stay a little longer."

"NO! I can't! I might not make it back!" I was afraid that my mind would betray me and choose to stay forever.

"Please, Elizabeth, you have to try. Just concentrate and think that you just want a couple more days. Nothing permanent."

Reluctantly, I tried. I squeezed his hands, probably a little too tightly, closed my eyes, and thought repeatedly about how I needed at least one more day away. Just one.

After a few minutes the nausea subsided, but I was afraid to open my eyes. My entire body felt numb, so I wasn't sure if I was still holding onto Gabe or not. I think I might have passed out.

"Please wake up, please please, please. Just open your eyes."

I heard a man's voice. It was pleading for me to wake up. At first, it came through as only a whisper, so I wasn't sure who it was. Eventually, the voice became louder and more familiar.

I opened my eyes to find Gabe hovering over me. Relief instantly washed over his face when he saw me waking. After he gave me all the hugs and sweet kisses all over my face, he explained that I did pass out. He didn't know what to do, so he brought me back to his apartment, laid me in his bed and spent the last few minutes trying to wake me up.

It only took me a few minutes after I woke up to feel normal again. My nausea was completely gone. I don't know how I knew, or what exactly changed, but I just knew that I was able to successfully delay going home and that it wasn't permanent. As much as I want to stay, and will stay soon, my heart just wasn't ready yet, and I think that will be the key to all this. When I know in my heart that it is the right time, it will happen.

I explained this theory to Gabe and he thought it made sense. We both agreed that we were now together on borrowed time, as we were not sure how much longer I had to stay. We needed to conclude this conversation before we did anything else.

"What exactly did you mean when you said you can't go back yet?" Gabe just jumped right in with a heavy-hitting question. I wasn't sure if he would have caught on to that. It could have easily meant to him that I wanted to spend more time with him, but he knew better.

"I just…I mean, I feel…I don't know if I can say it out loud."

"If you don't say it out loud, it doesn't have to be true yet." It's like he had a front-row seat to my thoughts.

"Yeah, pretty much," I admitted. The tears came back.

"But you know, in your heart, your decision has already been made." He was right. My heart knew the truth. My head knew the truth. I just couldn't speak the truth.

I nodded to acknowledge he was right, and then I cried. Gabe held me until I couldn't cry anymore.

When I found my voice again, I asked, "Tell me, what is it going to be like when I stay?"

I feel like I already knew the answer, but everything sounded better coming from him.

"Well…" he started, and then took a minute to finish his answer, searching for the right words. "You are going to end up somewhere you have no control over. My internal alarm will send me to you, and I will waste no time finding you, because I have missed you so much, but I will also know that you will need me. I will take you in my arms, and greet you with a comforting kiss on your forehead. You will be sad, and probably be crying, which is understandable. You just said your last goodbyes to your mom, dad, and best friend. As difficult and heartbreaking as that was, you also understand that it was the right thing to do and that it just makes sense. Your quality of life back home has deteriorated, and you all realized and have accepted that it was never going to improve, because your body won't stop travelling, despite all your efforts to stop it or slow it down. At this point, I will hold you, and console you for as long as you need. When your tears stop flowing, and you have made peace with what just happened, it is only then that I will tell you how much I love you, and that I am ready to start our adventure together, but only when you are. Eventually, you will tell me that you are ready, and that is when I will take your hand, and take you with me, to start our life together."

"OK," was all I could say. All I needed to say.

Hours later, I left Gabe.

As promised, I came back home.

PREPARATIONS

L ast night was bittersweet.

It has been about two weeks since my last entry, so I have been home for a little under a month. I wish I could say I am feeling better, but I am not. Walking has become almost impossible because my legs have become so weak. Dad brought home a wheelchair for me to make getting around easier for all of us. If it were up to Dad, I would remain in bed, but being brought to the living room where I can see Mom and Dad all day just makes me so much happier.

My appetite hasn't changed. I'm only hungry sometimes, and even then, I can't manage to eat much. Mom was able to find a protein drink that doesn't suck too much, so I try to drink that throughout the day to try to maintain the little energy I have.

I know it all sounds super depressing, but I am doing my best to keep my spirits up.

A few days ago, Lotus came by to spend some time with me. I took advantage of having her here and called for a family meeting. When we were all gathered, they looked to me to start the conversation, but I just didn't know how to begin. How do you tell everyone you love, that basically, you are choosing to leave forever, that you are not choosing them? I felt selfish and ashamed. They all watched me for several minutes as I tried to find the right words to start.

"Liz, it's ok, you can say it, you need to say goodbye." Lotus had my back one last time.

I nodded and started crying. We all started crying. After a few minutes, I tried to ease the tension by saying that I wasn't leaving right now, so all the tears were unnecessary. After we all calmed down, thanks to Lotus breaking the ice, I was able to discuss everything.

I explained that the last thing I wanted to do was to make this decision. I made them understand that leaving is going to be the hardest thing I will ever do and that I don't want to say goodbye. They already know that I am strong and healthy when I am away, so choosing to live the rest of my life in good health, instead of staying here and suffering was understandable to them. I mentioned that I no longer want to be a burden. Mom got a bit mad at me and said that I could never be a burden to her, but of course, she was going to say that. I told her that I knew she and Dad loved me and had shown me that every day, but their entire life has become taking care of me. I don't want that for them anymore. Even Lotus is missing out on a lot of experiences at school because she keeps coming to see me. I had to make them understand that I am not only choosing this for myself but for them too. I made them all promise me that when I am gone, and after they are finished being sad, they will start living life again. I would love for Mom to go back to work where she thrived. Love for my parents to rekindle their relationship. Love for Lotus to experience all student life has to offer and to go after her dream job.

It was important for me to get all this out and say what I needed to say. I may travel tomorrow, or I may have many more weeks, or even months left at home, but if I left in my sleep, like I have done a few times before, without saying a proper goodbye, I would never forgive myself. They needed to know exactly how I felt, and also that I was going to be ok. I told them my plans, about the life that I will build with Gabe. I assured them that I wasn't going to be alone and that I was going to be safe and loved.

After I said everything I could think of, everyone else took turns saying their goodbyes. It was all so emotional, and there was more crying. Mom and Dad both took turns telling me that they are proud of everything I was able to accomplish, despite all my setbacks, and how they are proud of the person I have become. Lotus reminisced about our good times and told me how much our friendship meant to her. Honestly, it felt like a funeral, celebrating my life, before I go, instead of after. Highly recommend.

We didn't know how much time I had left until my next trip, so we all decided to throw Lotus and myself a double birthday party the next day, to celebrate our nineteenth birthday, since I was away for both mine and hers. That was last night. Mom made both mine and Lotus's favourite cakes. Dad went crazy decorating with balloons, banners and streamers.

It was a quiet evening for a party, but I think we just all wanted to be together. We did a lot more walking down memory lane, recalling past events, and all the funny things that happened. We tried to keep the conversations pleasant and joyful. We already had our depression party the day before, after all, when we said our goodbyes.

On that note, it is hard to say goodbye, without actually leaving. It just doesn't feel real, or final.

Last night was bittersweet because it was such a lovely time, but it will be the last time Lotus and I celebrate our birthdays together, and I believe it might actually be the last time I see Lotus. When my parents went to bed, we further reminisced about things we dared not to talk about in front of my parents. We laughed for hours and then cried for a few too. She left this morning. We hugged for as long as time allowed us, and when I started to say goodbye, she stopped me and said that we already did that, and she didn't want to hear it again. She told me she loved me, I told her I loved her too, and then she left.

Mom spent all day cuddling with me on the couch. Dad sat with us too and got us whatever we needed. I asked my parents if they wanted me to figure out what to do with all my stuff. Normally, you would pack all your belongings and bring them with you. My parents told me they would take care of it for me. I am going to miss all my band T's, albums, and a few other cherished objects I collected over the years. What upsets me most is not being able to bring even a single picture with me. Gabe and I have been trying to bring objects with us when we were experimenting with our travels, but it has never worked. All I will have are my memories and mental images of my parents and Lotus. In the end, I am grateful to even have that. I appreciate that not everyone has the luxury of time or gets to say goodbye. I am so thankful for the past few days. It was a gift.

DEAR MOM
AND DAD

This will be my last journal entry.

I can't tell you how, but I know I am leaving today. By the time you find my journal, find this entry, I will have already called you to me, to let you know I was leaving for the last time. We would have said our last goodbyes, and I would have asked for you to stay with me until I was gone. Knowing Mom, she would ask to hold me until I left, and I would have welcomed it.

Mom, I hope this journal is everything you were hoping for. I know I complained *a lot* when you first gave me this task, but in the end, I am grateful for it. Besides documenting all my adventures, writing has become therapeutic to me. You provided me with an outlet I didn't know I needed. Writing about what has happened has helped me sort through some difficult situations and emotions. It showed me when I became the villain in my own story, and guided me back to a place where I could once again empathize and grow.

If you want to skip, or at least gloss over some parts of it, I wouldn't mind. You may also want to give Dad a redacted version of it to read. You know how Dad gets about boys.

Dad, I think you should take Mom to a hockey or football game. Make her wear matching jerseys, just like we did, and buy her an obnoxious foam hand, or a funny hat too. Kiss her on the jumbotron, and buy her a hotdog. Ok, maybe the hotdog would be too much for Mom. Just because I am gone, it doesn't mean our traditions can't continue. I am going to look for a sporting event where I am moving to, and I promise to keep our traditions alive on my end.

Mom, Dad. I know I gave you a hard time for many years, and I am sorry. I know many times I accused you both of treating me like a criminal on house arrest. That could not have been easy to hear. I may not have understood your sacrifices then, but I am leaving understanding it now. I just want to say thank you, for looking after me, when I was too stubborn or naive to take care of myself.

I will miss you so much, and I know you will miss me too, but please, I don't want you to be sad for me. Know that I am starting a new adventure, a new journal entry, and I am excited about this. I get to start a new life with a man who loves me just as much as I love him. I am in good hands and forever will be with my partner, my protector, my guardian, my Gabriel.

I'll love you forever.

Love,

Elizabeth

EPILOGUE

We said goodbye to our dearest Elizabeth for the final time a few days ago. We knew this day would come and we have been preparing for it, for what feels like too long, but nothing truly properly prepares your heart for losing your child.

Although she was stolen from us too soon, we knew that for the last ten years, she was with us on borrowed time, so we never took for granted every holiday, birthday, or any moment we had with her, good or bad, easy or difficult.

I honour my daughter by writing this final entry in her journal. It was given to her to record her many fantastical stories. Or perhaps they were vivid dreams she had while she lay so still in her comas. We believe that she believed this other life she led was real, and in the end, we chose to let her believe that, to help make her passing as peaceful as possible.

I could set her stories straight, and explain her tumour and her diagnosis, but I want to honour her life as she lived it, as difficult as it was for us. She couldn't deal with her reality, so she made a new one. She became a traveller and was able to find an escape from her everyday hardships and pain. In the end, isn't that what we are all looking for? A way to make life easier, and more enjoyable?

She matured, fell in love, and dealt with many difficult situations while she was *away* from us. Who are we to tell her that her experiences aren't real because we were not there to witness them? If you feel an emotion so deeply, but do not share it with others, that emotion is still true to you.

She didn't believe she was dying. She was convinced that she was destined for a life elsewhere, and I want to believe she is doing that now, living her next, best life. I'm not a religious person, and I don't know what to believe about what happens to us when we die, but I want to believe Elizabeth's version. I can't accept that she is gone, but I will choose to believe that she is somewhere healthy and happy, with her Gabriel, who guided her into her next life.

I share her journal with you, to celebrate my Elizabeth, and to share her message. Whether she was aware of it or not, she has taught me that life really can be what you want it to be. We may not be able to change certain aspects of our lives, like a terminal diagnosis, but we can choose how we live with it. She chose wonder, adventure, joy, and love.

We love you too, Elizabeth, forever, and ever...
Love Mom

Printed in Great Britain
by Amazon

51385825R00139